INSIGHT

Rendezvous with God – Volume Four

Bill Myers

FIDELIS
PUBLISHING

*Discussion questions have been included
to facilitate personal and group study.*

Fidelis Publishing®
Sterling, VA • Nashville, TN
www.fidelispublishing.com

ISBN: 9781956454420
ISBN: 9781956454437 (ebook)

Insight: A Novel
Rendezvous with God Volume Four
Copyright © 2023 Bill Myers

Order at www.faithfultext.com for a significant discount. Email info@ fidelispublishing.com to inquire about bulk purchase discounts.

All Scripture quotations are from the Holy Bible, New International Version®, NIV® Copyright ©1973, 1978, 1984, 2011 by Biblica, Inc.® Used by permission. All rights reserved worldwide.

Published in association with Amaris Media International

Cover designed by Diana Lawrence
Interior layout/typesetting by Lisa Parnell
Edited by Amanda Varian

Manufactured in the United States of America

10 9 8 7 6 5 4 3 2 1

Graham Cooke:

Whose wisdom and insight have impacted my life.

☙

"Whoever believes in me, as Scripture has said,
rivers of living water will flow from within them."

Jesus Christ

☙

PART ONE

CHAPTER
ONE

"WELL, DOC, IT'S an honor to have you on board."
Assistant Warden Stamph, adjusted his chair to better
see me over the stacks of paperwork on his desk. He was
a compact man with thick bifocals, shaved head, and a
collar two sizes too small. His office smelled of old wood
and too much aftershave. "I tell ya, a fancy professor like
yourself willing to teach my boys a little literature, it don't
get any better than that."

"Thank you," I said. "It's great to—"

"I've been reviewing your list of recommended reading." He tapped the paper in his hands.

"Good, I think you'll see—"

"And Lizzie, my secretary, she's quite, what do you call
'em, a 'bibliophile'? She's read most all of this stuff."

"Then I'm sure she'll—"

"*Catcher in the Rye?*"

"Yes. A great coming-of-age—"

"All about rebellion, is it not?" Before I could answer,
he gave a throaty chuckle which turned to a brief cough.
"Trust me, we got enough of that here."

"Actually, it's not—"

"Same with this, *1984*. They'll make *us* out to be Big Brother and we've already got plenty of noncompliance as it is."

I watched as he went down my list of carefully selected novels for my Introduction to Literature class I'd soon be teaching here, in the Snohomish Correctional Institute for men.

"*Huckleberry Finn*?"

"Many, including Ernest Hemingway, feel it's one of the greatest American—"

"Uses the *n*-word, right?" He looked at me over his glasses, then grinned. "Don't get me wrong, the taco eaters would love it. But as you'll see, we're sitting on a powder keg between them and the Afros."

"It's not—"

"And Toni Morrison's, *Beloved*. Never heard of her."

"It's the story of black oppression in—"

"Nope."

I took a deep, silent breath. After my far-too-public debacle on late night news (redefining the term *pariah*) and my forced resignation from the university, this was the only employer who agreed to hire me. And, given my massive mortgage, medical bills from the unconventional birth by my niece, not to mention our special visits to an infant cardiologist or two (without insurance) well, if he wanted me to teach a class on Spiderman, I was all in.

"Do you, does Lizzie have any suggestions?" I asked.

"Yes, we do."

I waited, assuring myself it would be all right.

"*War and Peace.*"

I was wrong. "*War and Peace?*" I said. "I'm afraid that might be a little weighty for an introductory course to—"

"Written by some Russian, right?"

"Yes. Leo Tols—"

"So everyone agrees."

"Agrees?"

"Everybody hates Russia."

"I'm sorry, I don't quite—"

"Nothing creates unity like a common enemy." He waited. But only seeing confusion in my face, he explained. "We win, right?"

"Win?"

"War and Peace. America wins, right?"

I opened my mouth but no words were appropriate. None were needed as we were suddenly interrupted by a pulsing, brain-numbing alarm.

Stamph swore and rose from his desk to look out the window.

"What's going on?" I shouted over the noise.

"Nothing to worry about!" He reached for the window handle and began cranking it shut.

"Really?"

"Absolutely." He motioned to the sofa at the opposite wall. "You might want to sit over there, though. Farther from the window."

I quickly fumbled with my book satchel and moved as he strolled from the window to an adjacent wall filled with a dozen security monitors. Spotting something on the upper right screen, he stepped closer for a look.

"Is everything all right?" I tried to sound calm, despite a voice raised a good half octave.

"The library," he shouted over the alarm. "Looks like the Bible Study teacher collapsed." The phone rang and he crossed back to his desk to answer, "Speak to me."

Up on the monitor I watched as inmates in baggy beige coats and pants gathered around what must have been a fallen body. A guard, dressed in blue, moved in, trying to push them aside.

"Alright," Stamph shouted into the phone. "Call EMS and get him outta there." Then, "No, stay in lockdown." He threw me a glance, "I've got a visitor I want out, but we stay locked down 'til things settle. You know how they get. And send me Tag. I see he's there. No doubt responsible." He hung up and turned to me. "Sorry, Doc, we'll have to pick this up tomorrow."

"Is everything okay?" I repeated.

He flashed a reassuring grin. "Oh sure, sure. Looks like one of our faculty had a heart attack or stroke or something. Not to worry."

I tried to nod, but didn't quite succeed.

He turned back to the monitors, his smile fading. "Means I gotta find a replacement, though." He shook his head, swearing again, then paused and looked over to me. "You don't know anything about the Bible, do you?"

"Me?"

"Yeah, right," he scoffed at the thought. "A man with your education—an atheist, right?"

"Well, actually," I cleared my throat, "I've been reading quite a bit of it recently, but—"

"No way. You're yankin' my chain."

"No, uh . . . but that doesn't qualify me to—"

"People, some folks say the Bible is literature, right?"

"Actually, quite a few, but—"

His smile morphed into a grin.

"No," I said. "Seriously, I'm an English professor, I teach literature, not—"

"Which is exactly what the Bible is, right?"

"I—"

"You teach literature, you read the Bible, and you're not an atheist. Sounds like a slam dunk to me."

"Um, I—"

"Don't worry, you'll do great."

"But—"

"Even if you don't, who'll know the difference, right?"

CHAPTER

TWO

STANDING AT THE stern of the ferry on the way home, I gripped and regripped the cold, wet railing. *Call EMS . . . Sitting on a powder keg . . . You know how they get?* What had I gotten myself into? First day on the job and I'd nearly lost my life. Okay, maybe that's a slight exaggeration. Or was it?

"Rough day at the office?"

I turned to see Yeshua in his trademark robe and sandals, wind tugging at his hair.

I didn't bother hiding my sarcasm. "You think?"

He remained silent as we looked out over the channel—the water heaving in slow gray swells, clouds black and heavy with rain. After another moment, he spoke. "Remember, how I promised this would be your greatest adventure?"

I scoffed. "Lockdowns, teaching what I don't know, prisoners convicted for God knows what."

"And whom I deeply love."

"You love everybody."

"Like Father, like Son."

I looked back over the water. "You've been taking me on 'adventures' since the day we met. But this one—I'm not so sure."

"Have you ever been?"

He had me there.

"That's why it's called faith."

I nodded, not thrilled with the answer. "So, what's in store for me this time?"

"Only if you agree."

"Free will," I quoted a phrase he often used.

"Always."

"And if I say no?"

"I'll still love you. You won't reach your fullest potential, but you'll always have my love."

"And my fullest potential is . . ."

He tilted back his head and quoted, "*To become whole and complete, lacking in nothing.*"

I snorted at the impossibility.

He ignored me and continued. "All this time you've allowed the Spirit to grow inside you—love, peace, righteousness. And I couldn't be prouder."

I glanced down at the railing, never quite sure how to accept compliments from the Son of God.

He continued, "But it's all been from the inside out."

"Spiritual transformation," I said. "That's what you've called it."

"God's Spirit inside you doing the heavy lifting. If you tried it on your own, you'd just turn religious on me. And then we'd have to deal with all the judgment and pride nonsense."

I nodded, seeing that in enough people's lives, including my own.

"But now with my Spirit, you have rivers of living water inside you."

"Rivers of . . ."

"Life. My life. My love, peace, and whether you care to admit it or not . . . joy." (For the record, we had plenty of past discussions regarding my inner-Eeyore).

"My Spirit's inside you—pushing back on all the outside pressure."

"Your balloon analogy, from our first meetings."

"You remembered?

"Remember? I've been writing about it."

"Your book?"

"Books," I said, a bit sheepishly. "Looks like there'll be more than one."

He chuckled. "You've always been an overachiever. Just as well. And the sooner the better."

"Meaning?"

He gave no answer, but said, "It's time for those rivers of living water to flow out of you, so others can start drinking from them."

I paused, thinking it through. "Is that why Cindy, my ex, is coming home, thinking she can move back in with me?"

"Along with her boyfriend."

"Boyfriend!?"

"Spoiler alert. Sorry."

I bit my tongue, figuring it's best not to swear in God's company. "And my niece? And her baby? And that piece of work called, Chip?"

"And don't forget Darlene and Patricia."

"And this prison thing too?"

"Stay calm. Buckle in."

"You're dropping me in the middle of a roaring freeway telling me to stay calm!"

"Keep your arms and hands in the vehicle at all times."

"That's not very—"

"And whatever you do, don't get out and push."

"Push?"

"At the speed we're traveling, you'll only wind up hurting yourself."

"So what am I *supposed* to do?"

"Just believe."

"Believe?"

"Kick back and enjoy the ride. Let me do the driving."

I closed my eyes, searching for patience, when the ferry shuddered and lunged. I reopened them just in time to see a giant wave crashing down upon us. I reached for the railing but there was no railing. It vanished into the dark. *Dark?* I panicked, groping for anything until I found a rope stretched from the deck to the mast. *Mast?* I peered through the driving rain and saw we were back on the disciples' boat—in the middle of the night—in a raging storm! Yeshua was standing beside me. Not exactly standing. He was three feet away, outside the boat, standing on the water.

"Seriously?!" I shouted.

He shrugged.

Another wave washed over us. I came out of it choking and coughing. When I caught my breath, I turned to him and shouted, "We're back in Galilee!"

He pointed to the other side of the boat where his frightened disciples were huddled in the wind, yelling at the big man I'd come to know as Peter. He was straddled over the edge of the vessel, one foot on the deck, the other foot in the water.

"Are you out of your mind?" they were shouting. "Get back here! Don't be a fool!"

I called to Yeshua. "Is this where he walks on water?"

He motioned for me to keep watching as the men continued to yell, pleading for Peter to come to his senses.

Someone grabbed Peter's arm, but he yanked it away and turned back to the lake.

And then, not thirty feet away, barely visible through the wind and rain, I saw Yeshua again—motioning for Peter to come out and join him.

I turned back to where Yeshua had been. He was there, as well. "That's you!" I yelled.

He nodded for me to continue watching.

I turned to see Peter now standing with both feet on the water—not *in* the water but *on* it—just like the Yeshua beside me. He was clinging to the side of the boat for all he was worth, as it rose and fell with each swell, but clearly standing . . . while, in the distance, through the driving rain, the other Yeshua motioned for him to come out and join him.

The big man was terrified, but he was determined. Slowly, he inched his foot forward, testing the water's firmness, until he'd stretched it out enough to take a step. Now he had a choice. Put his weight on that foot and lean forward, or do the sensible thing and pull back.

The men continued yelling at him to do the sensible thing.

But, keeping his eyes riveted on Yeshua, he shifted his weight to the front foot and released his grip on the boat. The men gasped. Everyone froze, including Peter—as they watched and waited.

He remained standing.

The Yeshua beside me shouted, "That's my boy!"

Then, as unsteady as a toddler taking his first step, Peter brought his rear foot forward. Wind ripped at his robe, rain and water blew into his face, but he kept his eyes locked on Yeshua until both feet were together, side by side—separated for balance, but together. When it was clear he wasn't sinking, he stretched out his first foot, put his weight on it as before and moved ahead. Another wave broke over the boat drenching us. I expected the same to happen with Peter. But to my astonishment, he rose on the wave like a cork then settled back safely into the trough—as he completed his second step, then a third, each more confident than the last.

I turned to the Yeshua beside me. "That's amazing!"

"Want to give it a try?"

"Me?"

He grinned.

"We tried that once," I shouted. "Back on the beach, remember?"

"You were a rookie. Welcome to the majors."

"I . . . don't know how?"

"Neither does Pete." He nodded back to the scene before us. "Just keep your eyes on me."

"I don't—"

Suddenly I was standing on the water—exactly where Peter had been, between the boat and the other Yeshua.

Only now there was no Peter and it was the Yeshua who had been beside me.

"No problem, Will!" he shouted. "You've got this."

I saw a wave coming at us and braced myself. But, like Peter, when it hit, I simply rose and fell with it. I looked down to see I was actually standing on water. How was that possible? I searched for the logic—not to mention a little courage.

Yeshua read my mind and shouted, "You don't need those! Just believe!"

I looked up to him and he nodded in encouragement. Then, against all common sense (and the hope people don't drown in hallucinations), I moved my foot forward, slow and cautious, before putting my weight on it. The surface was more spongey than firm, like a foam mattress. But it held.

"There you go!"

I nodded. Took a breath. And then I took another step. Once again, it held.

"See!" he shouted. "A piece of cake!"

I started my third step when I heard the men shouting behind me. I turned to see a killer wave coming directly at us.

"No!" Yeshua shouted. "On me! Keep your eyes on me!"

But the wave was huge. I wiped the water from my face and looked down. *What am I doing?*

"Me, Will!" Yeshua shouted. "On me!"

I was no Peter. I couldn't do this.

The wave hit and covered me. When it passed I was no longer on top of the water. Not entirely. I'd sunk to my calves. I panicked, trying to pull them up, but I only sank deeper until the water wrapped around my knees. Then my thighs.

"Will!"

I kept sinking. The water was at my waist. "Help me! I can't . . ." Then my chest.

I kicked and thrashed, but my coat had become a straitjacket, my shoes lead weight until, despite every effort, I was dragged under. I looked up to the surface moving farther and farther away. There was nothing I could do . . . until I felt a hand grab my wrist and pull.

Instantly, I was back on the deck of the ferry, gasping for breath, my hands clutching the railing. I turned to Yeshua but he was gone. Only his voice remained, four fading words. "Why do you doubt . . .?"

CHAPTER
THREE

I'M NOT A moron (despite what you may have read— and, yes, I've been writing furiously ever since Yeshua suggested I give it a try). But the point is, I got the message. Loud and clear. When it comes to faith:

Eyes on Yeshua: good.

Eyes off Yeshua: bad.

It's simply a matter of where I decide to look—his promises or my circumstances. Couldn't be simpler, right? Vintage Yeshua. But making the choice, particularly in the midst of my own Category Five storms, was going to be tricky. I had way too much on my plate. Nevertheless, what's the children's riddle, "How do you eat an elephant? One bite at a time"?

And by the look of things, the first course would be my ex, Cindy. According to Amber's call earlier this morning, she was at the house waiting to greet me—with the absurd thought she could actually move back in.

Seriously? I wasn't the one who claimed our life was a cure for insomnia and ran off with some Aussie, boy toy seven years her junior. I wasn't the one who drained our life savings while generously leaving me the house with a sizeable second mortgage. And I certainly wasn't the one who ripped out my heart, set it on a dinner platter, and wished bon appétit.

But I would be the one who was civil and polite. I'd even offer coffee to her and Buster (seriously, that's his name) while listening to their world adventures . . . before unceremoniously throwing them out. Despite any so-called *rivers of living water*, there was no way she was spending the night, let alone moving back in.

So that was my first course. An easy appetizer. No problem. Or so I thought . . .

As I pulled into the driveway, I was surprised there wasn't any sign of the Porsche her Facebook said the man-boy purchased just for her. In any case, I parked, climbed out of my beater Honda and crossed through the muddy gravel to the back kitchen door. Once inside, I was greeted by the usual leaps, barks, and manic hysteria of Siggy, our golden retriever. And I'd not even shut the door before I was hit with the sweet, pungent smell of marijuana.

"Amber!" I called to my fourteen-year-old niece.

"Uncle Will?" Her voice came from her bedroom down the hallway. "What are you doing home?"

"What are you smoking?"

"What's that?"

"Marijuana," I said, passing through the dining room and into the hall, "the place reeks with it."

She stepped outside her bedroom, still wearing the sweats she sleeps in. And why not, it was barely 1:00 in the afternoon. "I don't smoke," she said.

I was not in the mood. "What you do to your own body is up to you, but to expose the baby?"

"I'm smarter than that."

"I know the smell, Amber. I teach college."

"Taught." She stepped back into her room as I approached. "Why would I smoke when there's a hundred ways to eat it."

"So now you're a connoisseur of pot? I'm no fool, Amber."

"You're doing a pretty good imitation."

"You'd think with a baby, you'd be more responsible." I arrived at her door and saw the usual Department of Health challenges—mountains of clothes, scattered baby paraphernalia, unmade bed. And there, sleeping in the bassinet, squeezed in the corner slept sweet Billie-Jean.

"At least open the window and air it out," I said.

"You're such an autocratic deposit."

"You mean despot. An autocratic—"

"Again with the mansplaining."

"I'm not—"

"What's it like to know everything in the whole, entire world?"

"A burden, and stop changing the subject. You have no idea how that stuff can jeopardize Billie-Jean's cognitive devel—"

I stepped back to avoid a face plant from the slamming door.

"Amber?"

Nothing.

"Amber!"

Repeat performance.

"We're not done here, young lady. You and I are going to have a serious talk."

I stood another moment. When it was obvious we'd quit communicating—at least until she needed something—I turned and stormed down the hall to my own bedroom/laundry room/office. (My original bedroom had become the nursery, yet to be used, thanks to the dozens of duplicated baby shower gifts still unreturned). I threw open my door and was hit with a concentration of the smell—accompanied by hazy, blue smoke. I switched on the overhead fluorescent which performed its usual flickering light show before staying on. And there she was. Under the covers, facing away from me toward the washer and dryer. Only her fragile, bare shoulders showed.

I stood stunned, unsure what to say. She saved me the bother.

"Will you turn off the light?"

I reached for the switch before catching myself. "Cindy? What are you doing here?"

She remained silent.

"Cindy?"

At last she turned under the covers to face me. Her thick, honey-blonde hair had turned to straw. Her eyes sunken. She'd lost the weight she put on after we married, but it only added to an anemic, skeletal look. "Hi, Will." She sounded exhausted, her voice thin and raspy. "How you doing?"

It took me a moment to find my own voice. "Fine. And you?" I scowled at my politeness.

"Could be better."

"What . . . are you doing here?"

"Dying."

"Pardon me?"

"Cancer. It's gone to the lymph nodes."

I remained standing, trying to comprehend.

"Doctors say it's down to a couple months. Maybe weeks." I could find no response and she turned back to face the washer and dryer. "Turn off the light, please?"

CHAPTER
FOUR

"SHE'S LYING."

"How can you say that? You don't even know her."

"I know you."

I moved the phone to my other ear. "What does that—"

Darlene continued, "She's run out of money and now her and her *G'day Mate* have found a free meal ticket."

"She's in a lot of pain."

"So she says."

"How can you be so jaded?" I pulled down my car's sun visor to block the light finally breaking through the morning mist.

"How can you be such a mensch?"

"A mensch?"

"Always leading with your heart."

"That's so untrue. I'm a grumpy old man."

"You're an iron-clad cream puff. And we all know how to play you."

"All?"

"Amber, Patricia, me, even Billie-Jean. And now your ex. And what about this Chester jerk?"

"Buster," I corrected.

"Why wasn't he there?"

"She says he's out on the Olympic Peninsula tracking down a shaman who has a special blend of herbs and mushrooms to—"

"Of course. No doctors, no chemo, just easy living in a beach house for free and smoking weed."

"How'd you—you've been talking to Amber."

"Doesn't matter. I know the type. And where is she sleeping? No, let me guess, your laundry room."

"I don't mind the sofa. And it's not like she'll be here forever."

"Just until she dies or you die or they bilk you out of everything and move on. Get rid of her, Will. Today, tomorrow, the sooner the better. And if she doesn't leave, call the sheriff, or your lawyer friend."

"Darlene . . ."

"I'm telling you, she'll suck you dry. She did it once, she'll do it again."

"And if she's really sick."

"Get a doctor's report. Better yet, bring Patricia, your girlfriend, over."

"Patricia is not my—"

"Actually, that's a great idea. Do it this Sunday. When I'm over there fixing you and Amber dinner, invite Patty over; ask her to do a quick checkup."

"I'm not sure that's such a great—"

"I gotta go. Some kid's outside my office boo-hooing about the grade he deserves. Trust me on this, Will. Throw her out now, while you still can." Before I could answer, she hung up.

That's one thing I admired about Darlene. Actually one of many. She never hesitated to speak her mind. Whether it was her disdain for Patricia, who she felt was the poster child for everything wrong with religion, or her insistence that I was clueless about raising a teenage girl, let alone her baby. Still, she was always there. While everyone offered sympathizing lip service to Amber over the death of her mother and oohed and aahed over her newborn, only Darlene stepped in to hold the lost woman/child's hand, and occasionally the hand of her equally lost uncle.

I took the Highway 2 exit off I-5 and then south on 9 toward the Snohomish Correctional Institute for my first official day of teaching hardened convicts. That in itself was enough to keep my stomach churning all night. And pretending to be a Bible scholar? Please. Then, of course there was this minor problem of my ex-wife, sleeping in my bed with her boyfriend, where she expected to die.

Yeshua was not exaggerating when he said it would be an "adventure."

Had I planned to throw Cindy out last night? You bet. But that was before our second conversation, almost as brief as the first—when she explained they'd run out of money scouring Europe and Latin America for the right treatment. Cindy was never a fan of medical science; positive it was just a front for the pharmaceutical industry. Nature had a cure for everything—which explains why our struggle to have children was never properly addressed—and why I still have an aversion to any drink the color of green, brown, and yes, even blue, from past efforts to align my inner child with the harmony of the universe.

And, yes, during round two of last night's talk she agreed to stop smoking pot in the house. There were plenty of edible opportunities in Washington and would I mind picking some up on my way home from work? She appeared to be quickly fading and in a lot of pain, so I suggested we talk more in the morning. But when morning came, she said it conflicted with her internal clock and could we wait until my return in the afternoon? Against my better judgment I agreed.

Some things never change.

Do I sound resentful? Believe it or not, I'm not as bad as I had been. For over a year her running off was all I could think of. Then came Christmas and the beginning of Yeshua's special guest appearances. With them, through no fault of my own, I began changing. The more I hung out with him, the greater those changes became. His love was like some supernatural virus that had infected me and just kept spreading. Was there a cure? I suppose. But that would mean cutting myself off from him—something, despite my whining, I could not bear. But when would all this end? Would I just keep changing until I became the world's biggest doormat—some *mensch* letting anyone and everyone wipe their feet all over me?

"Hey, Will."

I blinked and was standing beside Yeshua on a dirt path. It ran along a dozen peasant homes, walls made of stone and plaster. As usual, he was surrounded by a crowd. And, as sometimes happens, they all moved in slow motion, like the minute hand of a clock—since, as he was fond of pointing out more than once, "time is relative."

"She has an interesting point," he said.

"Who?" I asked, trying to get my bearings. "What?"

"Darlene. On the phone."

"You heard that?"

"Omnipresence has its perks."

I frowned but wasn't surprised. "Is she right?" I asked. "About me being a mensch?"

He chuckled. "An interesting word. But it's true, you have started looking at others as more important than yourself."

"But . . . is that a good thing? I mean it won't be making it into any of those self-help books."

He cocked his head at me.

I explained, "Low self-image, not a popular topic."

"How can you have a low self-image when you were created in *our* image?"

My frown deepened.

"It's not about lowering *your* self-image, Will. It's about raising *theirs*.

I started to answer but wasn't sure how to respond.

Seeing my confusion, he smiled. "Hold that thought." He motioned to a young man directly in front of us—early twenties, neatly trimmed beard, wearing expensive robes, the outer one rich purple. "He was just asking what it takes to inherit eternal life."

I nodded and suddenly we were back to normal time as Yeshua turned to answer him. "You know the commandments: Don't murder, don't commit adultery, don't steal, don't bear false witness. Honor your father and mother."

The young man answered, as much to Yeshua as to the surrounding crowd. "I've done all those things since I was a child."

"Good," Yeshua said, "that's good. Then you're only lacking one thing."

"And that is . . . ?"

Holding the young man's eyes, Yeshua softened his voice. "Sell everything you own and give the money to the poor. That's when you'll have treasure in heaven."

The kid scowled, his countenance darkening as he glanced away to the crowd.

"And when you've done that," Yeshua added, "come and follow me."

The young man shifted, no longer letting his eyes meet Yeshua.

But Yeshua was in no hurry. He said nothing, waiting for the man to turn back to him. When he did, Yeshua spoke even more quietly. "How hard it is for the rich to enter the kingdom of God. It's easier for a camel to go through the eye of a needle."

The kid struggled to hold his gaze but again looked away.

Yeshua waited in the silence . . . until the young man began to slowly shake his head. Then, without a word, he turned and walked away.

The scene slowed to another near-stop.

I cleared my throat. "That was some harsh truth."

Still watching the young man, Yeshua replied, "That was love."

"But . . . how do you know the difference?" I said, thinking back to Cindy. "Between truth and love?"

"They're the same."

"For you, maybe. But what if I'm just being hard out of spite or anger."

"It's never a problem."

"Not for you."

"Not for anyone. Not if you hold the other person in higher esteem than yourself. When you do that, you'll always be acting in their best interests. And it will always be in love."

I looked down, thinking.

"If you can't wait to confront someone, no matter how great the truth, it's best to pause and reconsider. But if the last thing you want to do is to challenge them—" he nodded toward the young man, "then the chances are you're acting out of love."

I paused, then cut to the chase. "So, is she going to die?"

"We're all going to die."

"Thank you, Mr. Obvious."

He cut me a look. I glanced away, chagrined at my disrespect.

"That's Lord Obvious," he answered.

I looked back and saw his trademark twinkle. Nodding to the young man, he added, "The field is full of both wheat and weeds. In the beginning you can't tell the difference. That's why a wise farmer waits and watches. If he's too eager to judge and start pulling what he thinks are weeds, he may wind up destroying the good seed."

"But you've already called him out," I said. "I just heard you."

"Did I?"

"Teacher?" Suddenly we were back to real time. One of his followers asked him, "If what you just said is true about camels and the eye of a needle, who can possibly be saved?"

Yeshua looked back to the departing kid. "Just because something is impossible with man doesn't make it impossible with God."

Sun flared in my eyes and I shielded them to see I was back in the car alone. But the lesson wasn't quite finished. As I approached the sign welcoming me to Snohomish Correctional Institute, I heard his final words. "My Spirit can do anything, Will. Anything."

I turned into the parking lot, took a deep breath, and blew it out. As was so often the case, my simple question had an answer far larger than I'd asked.

CHAPTER
FIVE

"AS LITERATURE, THERE is no book equivalent to it in the history of the human race. In fact, it is actually sixty-six books. Sixty-six separate books written by forty different authors over the course of nearly 2,000 years. And here's the beauty . . ." I held up the Bible, pausing to build suspense, then delivered the punch line: "Each and every book is in perfect harmony with the others!"

Bam! Mic drop. If that didn't grab them, they were dead.

By the look in their eyes, there was no pulse.

I adjusted the notes on my lectern, a battered music stand that kept slipping down. Light filtered through opaque, wire-meshed windows onto my five students dressed in tan, baggy pants, various degrees of matching shirts and coats, with everyone wearing white, crew-neck undershirts. As far as I could tell, their expressions hadn't changed since they first shuffled into the room, a cramped library smelling of old books and disinfectant.

Okay, I thought. *I'm a professional instructor, I can handle this. I'll go for a more interactive approach. Something personal.* I grabbed one of the folding chairs in front of me. After a glance for approval from the guard at the door— a tall man, easily NBA material—I left the security of my notes, pulled the chair across the linoleum floor into the center of the room, and sat on its back.

"But before we get into all that," I said, "let's get to know each other first. In fact, let's bring it in." I motioned to the two black men sitting against the wall to my left— one, a big, brooding fellow, well over six foot, and the other, equally as cut but smaller, who wore an embroidered Muslim skull cap. "Why don't you fellows, move in closer to . . ." I nodded to the scrawny, white kid sitting dead-center before me.

"Sparky," he volunteered—with such eagerness he was obviously vying for teacher's pet.

I turned right and gestured to the remaining two men sitting at the opposite wall. Both were Hispanic—one with a beard and flowing black hair to his shoulders, the other sporting a buzz cut and shiny scar tissue around his neck.

Like the other two, they simply stared. I'm not convinced they even blinked.

"I really don't think—" Sparky cleared his throat, his voice caught between manhood and puberty, "—that's really not a very good idea."

I was clueless, but his uneasy look convinced me not to press the issue. "Okay, well then . . ." I coughed slightly. "I've told you a little bit about myself. Before we get started, let's each share a little with the group about yourselves."

The man in the skull cap replied with an air of refinement, "We know who we are." Throwing a look to the kid he added, "Inside and out—right, Sparky?"

The boy forced a giggle.

"Right." Having no idea what that meant, I moved on, "But for me, to bring me up to speed—a little bit about who you are and why you're taking this class."

I looked at them.

They looked at me.

Only the quiet *whoosh* of the overhead air ducts broke the silence.

I turned back to the gentleman in the skull cap. "How 'bout you? What's your name?"

"Ahmed Jamil Tajik."

I repeated, "Ahmed Jamil—"

"Tag. People call me Tag."

"And why are you with us, Tag?"

"Amusement mostly."

"Amusement?"

His big companion snickered. Tag merely looked down shaking his head at my ignorance. I turned to the other wall. "And you, sir?" I asked the long-haired gentle-men. "Your name?"

"If thou was truly from God, thou wouldst have no need to ask."

"Pardon me?"

"You would know the truth and it would set you free."

"And the truth is . . ."

"Have I been with thee so long and ye have not yet known me?"

"Um . . ."

"Jesus Christ," Tag's companion swore from the other side of the room.

At least I thought it swearing, until the long-haired man bowed his head and replied, "At your service."

I wasn't sure if I nodded or what I did. Motioning to the inmate beside him, the one with the buzz cut and scar, I asked, "And your name?"

He gave no answer.

I waited until Sparky volunteered. "PK. His name is PK."

A ray of hope dawned. Patricia once called herself an MK, short for *missionary kid*, while at the same time she said PK stood for *preacher's kid*. It was a long shot, but I'd cling to any straw I could find, scar or not.

I waited another moment. When it was clear he wouldn't participate, I turned to the final student, Tag's companion, the big black man to my left. "And you are?"

Showing no expression, he muttered, "Hatch."

"Hatch?" I said, "Like batten down the hatches?" A lame attempt at humor.

"Like hatchet," he said.

"Hatchet?"

Still showing no expression, he raised his right arm—revealing a stub where a hand should be."

"Okay then," I covered my cracking voice with a cough. "Well, um, why don't we start off by looking at the Sermon on the Mount. If you'd open your Bibles to—" I came to a stop realizing only Tag and PK held Bibles in their hands. Undeterred, and refusing to show weakness (something I'd read inmates thrived on), I pressed forward. "Who wants to read the first twelve verses of Matthew 5 for us?"

No response.

No surprise.

"Any takers? Anybody?" I turned to my right. "PK?"

"He doesn't read," Sparky said.

"You're taking a literature class and you don't read?"

Tag called from the other side. "It's either that or breakfast duty. Rising at 4 o'clock, fixing the (insert expletive), then cleaning up after all the (insert more expletives).

"Okay, then . . . Well, PK, would you mind passing your Bible over to, um . . ." I realized I'd yet not asked the long-haired man with the King James's accent his name.

"Anointed One," he said.

"Anointed—"

"As in Messiah."

"Right. Well then, um, do you want to read for us?"

"If you have no objection, I'd prefer to recite from memory as it is one of my favorite discourses."

"Okay . . ."

He closed his eyes and began. "In the beginning when we created the heavens and earth, the earth was without form and—"

"Actually," I interrupted. "That's from Genesis. The Old Testament."

"And what do you have against the Books of Moses?" Tag asked.

"Yeah," Hatch agreed. "Ain't that where all the blood and carnage take place?"

For the first time PK spoke, his voice thick and gravelly. "Where that puke God of yours wipes out anyone who disagrees with him."

Tag shot him a look, "Such blasphemy only proves your lack of intelligence. They murdered their own babies, sacrificed them to idols."

"Um . . ." I threw a nervous glance to the guard who appeared unimpressed.

PK fired back, "Your God is a sadist."

Tag rose to his feet. "Allah, may his name be praised, is truth and mercy."

"Then Allah is a (insert another colorful explicative)."

Tag's face reddened, a vein on his forehead bulged.

"Children." Anointed stood. "Please . . ."

"How dare an infidel such as you blaspheme his holy name," Tag's voice was low and murderous."

"I'll blaspheme whoever I wish, boy."

It was Hatch's turn to rise. "Boy!?"

"If the noose fits—"

"My children!" Anointed repeated.

"Alright, fellas," the guard interrupted, resting his hand on his baton. "Looks like school's over for the day."

Despite the lethal looks, both sides seemed to respect the tall man—or at least his baton.

He motioned Hatch and Tag to the door. "You two, first."

Still sharing expressions of ill-will, they turned and shuffled out of the room. As they did, Sparky saddled up to me.

"Sorry about that." He gave a shrug. "But you know about the gangs, right?"

"Gangs?" I said, keeping half an eye on the two men as they exited.

"Blacks and Latins, they don't mix. At least you don't got any AB's."

"AB's?"

"Aryan Brotherhood. So that's a plus."

"What about you?" I asked.

"Me? I'm a neutron, neutral."

"I see. Well, thanks for coming today, Sparky."

"Of course." There was something so genuine and vulnerable about the kid, I liked him immediately. "And if you ever need any help with anything, well I kinda know this stuff a little."

"You know the Bible?"

He shrugged again. "A little."

"Sparky," the guard ordered, "you're next."

"Yes, sir," he answered, then turned back to me. "Great class, Preacher. Don't let them discourage you."

"Actually, I'm not a—"

"Let's go, son." The guard approached.

"Yes, sir." Sparky turned and headed for the door.

I watched him exit. Then to the guard I said, "Sweet kid."

"That's what lots of 'em say."

I wasn't sure of his meaning but said, "He says he's a neutral."

The guard chuckled, "Yeah, an equal opportunity provider." He called out to the other two waiting men. "Okay, Anointed, PK. Let's move."

The two Latins followed Sparky and headed out the door.

I motioned to PK. "Before he leaves, may I talk to him a moment?"

"Trust me," the guard said. "You don't want to."

"Actually, we might have something in common. PK. Any idea what that stands for?"

"Sure," he answered, keeping an eye on the two as they left the room. "Police Killer."

I blinked.

Seeing the color drain from my face, he laughed. "No, no. Not police *man*."

"Then . . ."

"Police *dog*."

"Dog?"

"He killed one with his bare hands."

"Ah," I said, not exactly feeling better.

CHAPTER
SIX

IN A STRANGE way it was almost like old times— Cindy and me unwinding after a hard day's work, sitting in matching recliners, looking out over Puget Sound as we watched the San Juan Islands turn purple then violet then black as the sun dropped from sight. This time, however, there was no Karl the cat. Since her return, he seemed to go out of his way to avoid her. Odd, since they'd been inseparable before she left. Instead of his annoying presence, we had something entirely different and a thousand times better. Billie-Jean who lay sound asleep in my arms. I never tired looking at her—those long lashes, the tiny fingers, and a peace that always seems to accompany her . . . at least when she slept.

Holding Billie-Jean I couldn't help but wonder how things might have been different if Cindy and I had a child of our own. If the depth of love I felt for this little one had been shared between the two of us. Could something that powerful have held us together? Yet, how many stories had I heard of desperate couples hoping a child would save their relationship when even that wasn't enough to overcome our Walmart culture that believes if my mate doesn't meet my needs I can exchange them for another. Still, as I held Billie-Jean, it was hard not to imagine how things might have been.

"You've changed."

I glanced to Billie-Jean under my slight paunch which I stealthily sucked in.

Cindy chuckled, shaking her head. After seven years of marriage, *stealth* with her wasn't my strong suit.

Justifying my weight gain, I said, "Darlene. You remember her from the university?"

"Darlene, the man trawler?"

"She comes over ever Sunday afternoon and fixes these incredible meals."

Cindy arched an eyebrow

"For Amber," I quickly explained.

"Hm-mm."

"I'm serious. She's taken her under her wing—now that her mother is no longer with us."

Cindy quietly nodded. "She was a good person, your sister."

"When she wasn't strung out on drugs."

She gave no response, an obvious agreement. "But you," she said. "Amber says you found God."

"More like he found me."

"And it shows."

I scoffed.

"No, it's true. You're not the same Will Thomas I left a year ago."

"Actually, seventeen months ago."

"Seventeen months, it's been that long?"

I wanted to add, *and two weeks and three days*, but figured that type of childish petulance was beneath me (even though we both knew better).

She smiled, a little sad. "You've kept track, how sweet."

I shrugged. Sweet wasn't exactly my motivation. More like anger and resentment. But I let it go and looked back out the window, watching in silence as the tide slowly returned, a steady line of dark water spreading across the mudflat.

After a moment, she spoke. "I forgot how peaceful this place was."

"You used to say it was boring."

"No, Will," she chuckled. "I said *you* were boring."

Touché.

"But you were always there for me," she said. "I'll give you that."

"And Buster?"

"He's young." She looked down. "He's got needs." I turned to her as she continued, "We always agreed to have an open relationship."

"Meaning?"

"Do you really think it takes two days and a night for him to connect with his shaman friend?"

"Maybe his shaman friend is out on some trek, collecting his . . . potions."

"She. His shaman friend is a she." I said nothing and watched as Cindy looked back out the window. "I'm sick," she softly said.

I quietly repeated, "And he's got needs."

She remained silent.

Should you be wondering if a part of me was thinking, *All right, payback!* you wouldn't be wrong. But there was another part, equal if not stronger: a rising pity. And, strangely enough, compassion.

We sat like that, in the silence, for a long time—each knowing the elephant in the room had to be addressed. Finally, with some reluctance, I spoke. "So . . . how long do you think you'll be staying?" When she gave no response I continued, "Tonight, of course, but what about tomorrow?"

She shook her head.

"Cindy . . ."

"I know, I know. And you're a champ for letting us stay."

Or chump, I thought.

"Just as soon as Buster gets back we'll sort things out. I promise."

"That's not exactly an answer."

She started to respond then broke into a fit of coughing—involuntary or not, I couldn't tell. Either way, it was painful watching it rack her body. When she finished and caught her breath she said, "It won't be long, I promise. If you want, I can sleep on the sofa. Buster won't mind sleeping on the floor."

I scowled. I'd not even considered the two of them sharing my bed. But of course, what other option was there? I silently sighed. Apparently one insult to injury wasn't enough. Make mine a double.

She looked back out to the ocean. "Remember when we used to race the incoming tide across those flats. Staying just ahead of the water?"

"You skipping and dancing along the edge."

She shook her head, musing. "Exerting my magical powers, using sheer will to slow it."

"Which you never did."

"Mother Earth is a stubborn broad."

I agreed. "She's used to having her way."

"And always catches up—eventually." I frowned and she explained. "Karma. What goes around comes around."

I nodded. But even then I knew the cycle could be broken. I'd experienced it firsthand. And, before I could catch myself, I was saying, "It doesn't have to be like that, you know." I cleared my throat and pressed on. "Someone can take the blame for all that, for all your failures. Take the blame and set you free from them."

Cindy cocked her head at me. I felt my face growing warm. What on earth had I just said?

With a gentle tease, she replied. "Look who's turning Billy Graham on me."

My eyes faltered and I looked down.

But instead of ridicule, she reached out and set a hand on my arm. "If it's working for you, Will, I'm glad. Really, I am."

Of course, I wanted to add, if it's working for me, it could work for anybody. And if she really was in the last days of her life, maybe she shouldn't rule it out. Maybe she ought to explore it a bit more seriously. But saying that would require courage or faith or whatever it was I lacked. Even saying that much left me both embarrassed and amazed.

Once again, silence stole over the conversation. How long we sat there, looking out at the water as darkness wrapped around us, I can't say. But when I finally turned back to her to ask if she was chilly, if she wanted a blanket, her eyes were closed and her chin rested upon her chest, breathing deeply in sleep.

ᑫᓄ

Buster did not show.

And what did I do about it? Nothing. Except go to Amber's room and convince her to get off the phone with Heart-Throb-Chip and help me move Cindy back to bed—not, of course, without the mandatory eye-roll and abundance of insight. "You know you can be a real hypocrite."

"Excuse me?"

"Hypocrite, that means actor."

"I know what it—"

"Pretending you don't love her."

"Pretending? That horse left the barn months ago."

"So what are you doing all this for?"

"Because she's sick. She needs help."

"Love is blind."

"What does that mean?"

She said nothing, letting me absorb the depth of her fourteen-year-old wisdom.

"Listen," I said, "there is no way on God's green earth that I still—"

"Absence makes the heart grow fonder."

"Amber."

"Love, love, love."

"Knock it off. It's over."

"Denial: a river in Egypt."

Knowing Amber's definition of a discussion was always to have the last word, I let it go.

We joined Cindy at her recliner and helped her to her feet. Despite her insistence she could make it on her own, we each took an arm and walked her down the hall to my laundry room/office/master bedroom/now guestroom.

Once we eased her onto the bed, I asked Amber if she'd mind helping her undress.

"Hypocrite," she said.

"Right." I turned for the door, "Academy Award winner."

"By the way, I figured it out," she said.

Ignoring my better instinct, I turned back to her.

"You don't have to sleep on the sofa anymore."

"Amber, there's no way I'm sleeping—"

"You can sleep in my bed."

"And where are you and Billie-Jean going to sleep?"

"At Chip's."

"Wrong." I stepped into the hallway.

She followed me. "You can trust us."

"Strike two."

"Honestly, you can be such a Nazi sometimes? A real Stalin Bolshevik!"

I continued down the hall. "Studying World War II, are we?"

She stopped, hands on hips and demanded, "Why can't I stay at Chips? Give me one reason why you won't let me."

"Why *I* won't let you?"

"Yeah.

I rounded the corner into the kitchen, but not before leaving my answer: "Love."

If she swore I was too far away to hear.

Twenty minutes later I'd set up yet another office—my third in the past six months, but who's counting (or whining). This time it was on the dining room table. I sat there with my laptop trying to focus on the next day's lesson for the prison. If the men wanted Old Testament, I'd give them Old Testament—particularly chapter one:

"God created mankind in his own image. In the image of God he created them, male and female."

A simple concept they could all grasp. Simple but powerful. The online commentaries called it *imago Dei*— the idea if we were each created in God's image, we should treat one another with honor and respect—regardless of race, creed . . . or gang. Not only honor each other, but in Sparky's case, honoring yourself.

Odd, the opposing gangs were certainly an issue, but Sparky's own lack of self-respect also haunted me. *An equal opportunity provider*, the guard said. It didn't sound like the prison stereotype of a weaker man being forced to have sex with a stronger one. Instead, it sounded more like, well there was no other word for it but *prostitution*.

Imago Dei. A long-shot for the prisoners to accept? In an environment of hate, power, lust, and fear? Was it even possible? No more than throwing my feet over the side of the boat and walking on water.

Okay, then. If Yeshua wanted faith, he got it. *Imago Dei* it would be. But there was another word that kept bubbling up in my brain:

Hypocrite.

Of course, Amber was wrong. My feelings toward Cindy had nothing to do with love; trust me on that. At least romantic love. Instead, they were mostly anger, bitterness, resentment and, well, I suppose we've all been down that road one time or another. But what about the other love? The type Yeshua kept speaking of? Forgiveness, mercy, kindness? They were there too. Sometimes simultaneously. *You're not the same Will Thomas I left a year ago.*

No, Amber was wrong. I wasn't a hypocrite. I was schizophrenic. Loving and resentful. Merciful and vengeful. How was that even possible? The question barely formed before my office wavered and I was standing in a thick grove of trees.

SEVEN

"I'M TELLING YOU the absolute truth: no one can come into the kingdom of God unless they're born of both water and of Spirit."

It was night and Yeshua spoke to a lone, elderly man dressed in expensive robes—not as fancy as the rich kid's I saw earlier, but definitely high class. Mottled moonlight filtered through the trees just enough for me to see the old fellow scowling.

Yeshua continued. "Flesh gives birth to flesh, but the Spirit gives birth to spirit."

The clarification did little to ease the man's confusion.

Yeshua tried again. "It shouldn't surprise you when I say you have to be born again. It's like the wind that blows wherever it will. You can hear its sound, but you can't tell where it comes from or where it's going. So it is with everyone born of the Spirit."

The old man shook his head. "What does that mean? How can it be?"

If Yeshua saw me, he gave no indication. Instead, he kept his vision fixed on the man. "You're one of Israel's teachers and you don't understand?"

The man held Yeshua's gaze, not offended, but not exactly pleased.

Yeshua continued, "Hear me carefully. I'm telling you what I know—and what I've seen."

"What you've *seen*?"

"And you still won't accept my words. If I tell you earthly things and you don't believe me, how can you possibly believe when I tell you about heavenly things?"

"What you've *seen*?" the man repeated.

Yeshua answered, "No one has gone into heaven except the one who came from heaven—the Son of Man."

The old-timer looked to the ground trying to absorb what he heard.

But Yeshua still wasn't finished. "It's like Moses lifting the snake up on the pole in the wilderness. In the same way, the Son of Man must be lifted up."

"Why? To what purpose?"

"So anyone who puts their trust in him can be saved and have eternal life."

The man's eyes shot back up to him.

Yeshua simply nodded, then added, "God loves this world so intensely he will sacrifice his one and only Son to save it. And anyone who believes in him will not perish, but live forever."

The poor fellow was more lost than ever.

Yeshua pressed in. "God didn't send his Son into this world to condemn it, but to save it. And *anyone*, who puts their trust in him will not be condemned. But anyone who doesn't trust him is condemned already."

"Why?"

"Because they don't believe in God's one and only Son."

Sadness filled with sadness. Or maybe it was pity.

Yeshua softly concluded. "This is the final verdict: Light has come into the world. But because of their evil deeds, people love darkness instead of light. They hate the light because they're afraid it will expose their evil. But whoever lives in truth . . ." Yeshua paused for emphasis. "Whoever lives in truth will come into the light so his behavior will be plainly seen by God."

The older man stopped moving—not completely, but slow enough to indicate Yeshua created another one of his "I-live-outside-of-time" moments. He turned to me and smiled.

I took my cue and approached. "That's quite a download."

Yeshua nodded and turned back to the man. "He's going to need some time to digest it. He's confused but he's hungry. And that hunger will be his blessing." Turning to me he grinned. "Just like someone else I know."

I blew out a breath of frustration. "Well, you're right about one thing. I'm completely confused about what's happening to me."

"The metamorphosis?"

"The what?"

"New truths, new realities—being born again can be a little disorientating."

"*Born again?* I thought that already happened? Back in January?"

"Your birth? Absolutely. But growing up takes time."

"You lost me. Again."

Even in the dim light I saw that trademark grin and sparkle in his eyes. Gathering his robe, he crossed to a fallen tree and sat, motioning me to join him.

"Tell me," he said, "have you ever stopped to consider the butterfly?"

"Another metaphor?"

"Metaphor, parables—kind of my thing. As an English prof, you know they can go deeper than literal explanations." I nodded and he continued, "The point is, butterflies don't start out as butterflies. They begin as caterpillars. Content to eat and crawl on their bellies. Eat and crawl. That's all there is to their life—until their metamorphosis. Until they're called into the solitude of their cocoon. And there, in the silence, dead to the world, everything about them becomes disarrayed, rearranged."

"Welcome to my life."

"Neither worm, nor butterfly. Yet, somehow, both."

"Schizophrenic," I said.

"Not a man of flesh. Not a man of Spirit. But both."

"Something is happening, I just can't explain it."

"You hear the wind but can't tell where it comes from or where it's going."

As realization dawned, I quietly quoted, "*So it is with everyone born of the Spirit.*"

"Exactly."

"And that didn't happen in January?"

"In God's eyes, yes. But it takes a lifetime for your soul to catch up."

"Soul? I thought we were talking about Spirit."

He chuckled. "May I borrow your pen?"

I patted my pockets. "Sorry, I left it on the table in my—"

Suddenly, we were back in the dining room. I briefly closed my eyes to get my bearings. When I reopened them, Yeshua was seated beside me, reaching for my computer. "May I?"

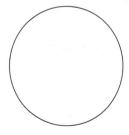 I nodded and he took the keyboard, quickly opening some graphics program (his computer learning curve was obviously faster than mine). He drew a circle on the left side of the screen.

"Remember when the boys asked me to sum up all the commandments; do you remember what I said?"

I nodded. *"Love God with all your heart, soul, and mind."*

"And?"

"Love your neighbor like yourself."

If he heard my pride in remembering, he didn't let on. "Okay, then. Let's break that down a little. What say we call this circle, your heart—all of your emotions, all of what you feel." I watched as he typed the word *Heart* inside the circle.

He drew another circle on the right of the screen, overlapping part of the first. "And let's call this . . . our logic center where we do all our thinking." He typed the word *Mind* inside it.

Continuing, he said, "The good news is we're not entirely emotion but we're not entirely logic, either."

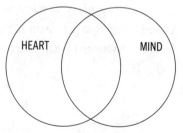

"A combination," I agreed. "Not totally Mr. Spock and not some fourteen-year-old niece."

He gave me a look. It was my turn to shrug.

He motioned back to the circles, a type of Venn diagram. "And that combination," he pointed to the center, "that's who you are; your character, your personality. Your . . ." Inside the shared area he typed the word *Soul*.

Looking on, I repeated, *With all our heart, soul and mind*.

"But there's one part missing," he said. "The part that makes you different from animals. And that would be . . ." He waited for

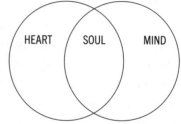

my answer but I was clueless. "Come on, Will, we just talked about it."

"Our . . . spirit?" I guessed.

"Exactly. Now some folks say soul and spirit are the same, but humor me on this," he said as he added a gray

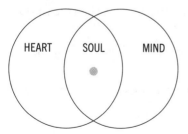

dot in the center of the diagram.

"Kind of puny," I said.

He nodded. "It's alive, but not complete. Like a human egg, an ovum. All the potential for full-grown life is there, but it will never happen unless it's fertilized."

"By?"

"The Spirit of God. Your spirit impregnated by God's Spirit. Pollinated. Creating a brand-new life."

"Born again," I half-whispered.

"Not by human flesh . . ."

"But . . . by your Spirit."

"Flesh gives birth to flesh, but Spirit gives birth to spirit."

He let the idea take root before continuing. "Sadly, many of my brothers and sisters stop at pollination; the rebirth happens but they grow no further. They think being born again is the end of the process, when in fact it's just the beginning. The Father and I still love them, they're our children, how can we not—but they'll always remain infants, constantly soiling themselves with their sin and self-centeredness."

"Again, welcome to my world."

He shook his head. "No, not any more. Your reborn spirit has been steadily growing inside you, Will. As with any newborn, it needs nutrition and you've had the wisdom to be feeding it."

"I'm guessing we're not talking about McDonalds and Taco Bell?"

"Flesh feeds flesh. But what does an eternal spirit need to eat?"

"Something eternal?"

"Like . . ." He turned to me, waiting.

I frowned, mulling over our times together, all he'd been teaching me over the months. I saw a glimmer of light. It was a long shot, but I gave it a try. "You?" I suggested. "I mean you call yourself the 'Bread of Life,' right?"

He grinned, obviously pleased.

I continued, "And the more I eat of you . . ."

"The greater your spirit grows." He added arrows from the first dot leading out toward the circles.

"Until God's Spirit begins replacing your old ways of thinking and your old ways of feeling. Until you're no longer the old William Thomas living by your

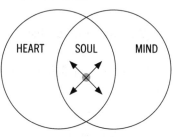

flesh, but the new William Thomas living by my Spirit."

I looked at the diagram, slowly marveling.

"And it doesn't stop there." He continued extending the arrows. "As you keep growing, our Spirit begins

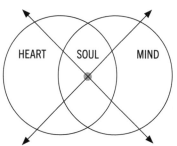

overflowing from you and onto the rest of the world."

I nodded, quietly repeating the phrase from our last conversation. *"Rivers of living water."*

"From your innermost being, that's right. Overflowing and soaking everyone you meet. Until . . .?" He waited for me to complete the thought.

"Until I'm loving my neighbor as myself." I continued staring at the chart. "And that's . . . that's what's happening to me? Why I'm doing things I don't even want to?"

"Except—" he tapped the screen, "the new you actually wants to."

"Even when it hurts."

He chuckled. "Even when it hurts."

"And the term for that?"

"Pardon me?"

"Is there some fancy, theological phrase explaining all this?"

"Yes, I believe there is."

"And that is?"

"We call it . . . *growing pains.*"

CHAPTER
EIGHT

"WHAT ABOUT ENABLING?" Patricia asked.

"Enabling?" I said.

"People need to learn to stand on their own two feet."

"Actually, she can barely get out of bed."

I adjusted the phone against my ear, once again wishing for one of those fancier cars with a built-in phone system to avoid hiding it every time I saw a State Patrol. The current fine is $136. I was thirty minutes from the prison. The morning fog had retreated into small pockets along the side of the freeway. Weather report said it was going to be a scorcher. When it got hot in Washington, even on the west side of the Cascades, it got hot.

So, was I going to enjoy my new job? A room filled with rival gangs who could attack each other at a moment's notice? A big man who'd cut off his own hand with a hatchet, another who killed police dogs, and a young kid who despised himself so deeply he sold his body to the highest bidder? What's not to like?

I'd gone over my lesson plan on *imago Dei* half a dozen times before the ferry even docked on the mainland—the joys of being a closet O.C.—which gave me plenty of time during the rest of the drive to obsess on the other major issue in my life.

I'd avoided talking to Patricia ever since Cindy arrived. Not because I was afraid of being judged—alright, there was that—how do you tell a super-religious person you're trying to impress that your ex has been sleeping over? She'd already seen enough burning embers from my past, why throw gasoline on the fire?

Truth is, Darlene sensed my attraction to Patricia almost before I did: "Why else would you drag your sorry butt out of bed and go to church with her?" she once asked. But it wasn't Patricia's fashion-model looks. To be honest, I thought she could add a few pounds to that bird-like fame. Nor was it because of her no-nonsense lifestyle. As a missionary kid whose parents served in Papua New Guinea, she saw no need to participate in frivolous trends or political correctness. Instead, it was her unwavering discipline and laser-focused commitment to God I admired, which is why I never understood Yeshua's insistence that *I* was to teach *her*, instead of her teaching me. It made no sense. Even less that the beautiful Elven Queen would give this bungling Frodo the time of day.

"How many nights has she slept there?" Patricia asked.

"Just two."

Death-like silence followed.

"Hello? Are you there? Patricia?"

"If she's as ill as she insists, she needs to be hospital-ized; at least receive medical treatment."

"Right," I said. "But she doesn't believe in Western medicine. Says when you stop calling it a medical *practice* she'll start taking it seriously."

"And encouraging that behavior, you don't think that's enabling?"

"I wouldn't exactly say—"

"Letting her sleep in your bed, do you think that's healthy?"

"Oh, no, she's not in my bed. I mean she is, but she's not sleeping with me, if that's what you're thinking."

"Why would I think that?"

"No, of course you're not. I just wanted to make sure you understood that—"

"So where do you and Darlene sleep?"

"I'm sorry? Where do we . . . I'm not sleeping with Darlene."

"When she goes out to visit you."

"That's not . . . Do you think we've been sleeping together?"

"Everyone knows her reputation. And the way she looks at you."

"The way she . . .?" I rubbed my forehead.

"No matter," Patricia said. "She invited me out to your place for dinner, Sunday."

"To check on Cindy."

"Yes. After the three of us go to church."

"Three?"

"You, Darlene, and me."

I blinked. "Did she agree to that? I mean she's not exactly a—"

"I told her it was the only way."

"And she agreed?"

"She'll do anything to keep her man."

"Her man? Patricia, I'm not—"

"There's my other line. Got to go. I'll see you Sunday, then."

"Patricia—"

"Try not to be late."

"Patric—"

The line went dead. I was a little slower hanging up. How was this possible? How had I, the world's worst communicator with the opposite sex, gone from having no woman in my life to having two, three counting Amber— well five, if you count Cindy and Billie-Jean. And in forty-eight hours all would be sitting around my table.

I mumbled a faint prayer, "I hope you're enjoying this."

In the lane directly beside me I noticed a State Trooper motioning to my phone and ordering me to pull over.

"Yes," I finished my prayer, "I bet you are."

CHAPTER
NINE

SECOND DAY IN class. Same students, same attitude. Except tensions may have been a bit higher. My first clue? Assistant Warden Stamph waiting in the lobby as my personal escort.

"Your safety is a primary importance to us," he said as we moved through security and headed down the hall. "Despite appearances, please understand you aren't in any type of danger."

"Excuse me?"

"I'd be lyin' if I said there's no talk 'bout a power shift happening."

"A power shift?"

"Within in the population. It'll have no effect on you or what you're teaching. But the men, they might be a little on edge. We've gone ahead and assigned you an additional correctional officer. Just in case."

"Correctional officer?"

"Guard," he explained.

And so, with that cheery bit of news in the back of my head, class began.

The first few minutes went as expected—combatants taking opposite walls—Tag and Hatchet to my left, PK and Anointed on my right—with Sparky in no-man's land directly in front of me. It wasn't until I started explaining *imago Dei* that the lecture began.

Not mine, Tag's.

"You can't chain someone up for hundreds of years, liberate them, then expect them to compete fairly with the rest of you."

I blinked, not entirely sure where he was coming from. "I, uh, I'm not suggesting—"

"Are you aware who said that? Lyndon Baines Johnson. LBJ, the 36th President of the United States of America."

I was about to tell my articulate, black Muslim student, I knew who LBJ was and, no, I was not the one who chained up blacks for hundreds of years, no more than he was the one chained—but I stopped when Yeshua appeared, silently sitting on the back of a chair beside him.

To be honest, I'd heard Tag's rhetoric on campus before, and to be even more honest, I'd grown weary of having my nose rubbed into something I wasn't guilty of. I owned no plantations, had several black friends (well, a few), and had never shown any prejudice I could think of. So please, stop blaming me about you being disadvantaged.

Oh, and while we're talking presidents, how about the 44th president of the United States, one Barrack Hussein Obama?

That's what I was thinking, but common sense, not to mention a preference for survival, suggested I keep my mouth shut.

Tag was on a roll. "You come around here with all your so-called Christian love when for centuries you treated us like property. And don't tell me you're not responsible. You're as guilty as your great-great whoever they were."

He paused long enough for me to finally squeeze in a word. I wanted to be careful but I was in no mood to be labeled a racist. Then, just as I opened my mouth, Yeshua called out from beside him, "Yes. Tell him, yes."

"What!?" I said.

Hearing my word and not Yeshua's, Tag said, "You heard me. Or are you deaf like all white folks your age?"

As a reminder that I didn't have to speak to be heard by him, Yeshua put his finger to his lips and tapped his temple. I turned back to Tag, planning to ask who was being more prejudiced; that, unlike him, I'd spent years of my life practicing Martin Luther King's dream of seeing all men as one color.

But Tag gave me no chance, plowing onward. "Or how 'bout that two-year study by Harvard and Stanford proving job applicants with white-sounding names are called back twice as often as black names?"

I'd not heard this and was about to say so, when Yeshua again motioned for me to stay silent. Not that I had much choice considering Tag's rapid-fire diatribe.

"Or that black women die four times more frequently than white women from pregnancy issues that can be prevented. Four times!"

Yeshua nodded to the fact while motioning for me to remain quiet.

"And infant mortality. Black babies in the United States die at twice the rate of whites. That's two times your rate!"

I felt my face growing hot. How long was I expected to silently sit and listen to the accusations; supposed facts I had no control over?

"And why in our lifetime are over 33 percent of black men incarcerated? That's one out of three? Compared to 6 percent of whites? You think we're just naturally more evil?"

"Or stupid," PK called from across the room.

Tag shot him a glare angry enough for the two guards—my NBA friend from before and a stout woman in her late thirties—to step from their respective walls as a reminder of their presence.

And still Yeshua insisted I keep quiet.

Tag shouted back at PK, "It's not about race, cholo. It's poverty. The poor are twice as likely to commit violent crimes!"

Anointed chimed in. "Blessed are the poor for they—"

"Shut up!" Tag turned back to me. "And why are we poor? Because we're lazy? Afraid of a good day's work?"

"That's two for two," PK shouted.

Tag ignored him, growing even more impassioned. "It's a vicious cycle. Poor neighborhoods mean poor schools mean poor education. High school dropouts go to prison sixty-three times more than college graduates! And who's to blame?"

I looked to Yeshua.

"Well," Tag demanded. "You've got nothing to say for yourself?"

At last, Yeshua nodded, giving me permission to speak. But speak what? *What am I supposed to say?* I thought.

"Ask him to forgive you," Yeshua said.

"Forgive *me*?!" I blurted.

The words set Tag back. My response left him as defenseless as it left me. "What?" he demanded. "Why'd you say something like that?"

Yeshua spoke another word, only one: "Love." He motioned me to say it.

I stared at him. He nodded.

Finally, I stammered, "Love."

"Love!" Tag shouted. "You showed us no love!"

Yeshua nodded at me and spoke. "Which is why you, Will Thomas, are guilty."

I could only look at Yeshua, mouth ajar. If I wasn't in front of the men, I would have had a major argument. Instead, I could only stare.

Tag followed my gaze. "What are you looking at? What are you saying?"

"Tell him," Yeshua said.

I kept staring, trying to grasp the fact. Was it possible? Was I, by staying uninformed, by doing nothing, partially responsible?

"Tell him," Yeshua repeated.

I swallowed and took a moment. "You're right," I finally said. "My lack of love makes me . . ." I still couldn't say the word, so I softened it with another ". . . culpable."

There was no sound in the room except the blood pounding in my ears. Tag looked at me like I was a crazy man. No argument there.

With plenty of rage left, he shot back, "I'm not talking about love. Look around this place. It's about power. Everything here, everything in the world is about who has power."

"Yes," Yeshua agreed.

I closed my eyes.

"Tell him, yes."

My reply was hoarse but I finally said, "Yes."

"Are you playing me?" Tag demanded.

"What? No." I looked back to Yeshua who simply sat and watched.

"Love," Tag snorted in contempt. "Woman talk. All emotion, no logic."

I kept my eyes glued to Yeshua who wasn't giving clues.

Tag continued. "In Islam, Allah, may his name be praised, is logical. One plus one equals two. You do evil, you pay for it. Like gravity, you jump off a cliff, you hit the ground. That is how the universe runs. But you Christians, for you, one plus one equals a hundred, a thousand. A million. All your logic is gone because of what you call 'love.'"

At last, Yeshua spoke. But, once again, not the words I expected or wanted to hear. "Yes," he said, "tell him, yes."

What was he talking about? I wanted to argue, and planned to as soon as we got alone, but as always, I knew something was up. So reluctantly I agreed and said, "Yes." Having no idea where we were going, I kept an eye on Yeshua, waiting for more. But that was it. He simply nodded and motioned for me to continue.

Continue? With what? If Tag was right, Yeshua was the illogical one. I kept looking at him, waiting. But he gave no defense, no rebuttal. Instead, he raised his arms, the sleeves of his robe falling to his elbows, so his hands were visible. Opening his palms, he showed the shiny scar tissue grotesquely filling where the holes had been.

Realization swept in and I turned to Tag. "Yes," I repeated, "love is illogical." With a strange boldness I'd never felt before, I continued, "It was totally illogical for God to let us kill his Son."

Tag scowled.

I continued. "When I jump off a cliff, it makes no sense for him to be the one to hit the ground—to take my punishment." I swallowed again. "Or to take yours."

Tag bristled. "Mine! Why would he do such a thing?"

I glanced to Yeshua, but already had the answer. "Love."

Tag shook his head in disgust, then pointed across the room at PK. "And him? No matter how many died on the streets from his bad smack? You tell me he's still loved? Or Sparky?" He motioned to the boy. "How many homes you burn down?"

Sparky giggled and shifted in his chair.

Hatch weighed in, "And him whorin' and all; you sayin' that don't count?"

"You got the cash, he's your boy," PK said.

"Or girl," Tag said. "Ain't that right, Spark?"

Another giggle. "Gotta keep the customer satisfied."

Before I could catch myself, I turned to Sparky. "He died for you too, son."

He squirmed and looked away, mumbling, "Thanks, I'm good."

Maybe it was Yeshua's hands or maybe it was something else—like that Spirit he talked about. Whatever the case, I turned back to Tag. "If you knew how deeply loved you are, the logic you demand, the power you want, it would mean nothing." I looked over to PK and Anointed and repeated myself, "Nothing at all."

Hatch spoke again, his voice darker. "And if we used that power to crush you?"

Tag nodded. "He could break your neck before you had a chance to move."

I focused on Hatch; my boldness as strange as my compassion. "You could crush my body—but not my love."

Hatch held my gaze, a type of showdown—until Tag snickered and slapped him on the back, giving him an excuse to look away. "He's crazy. Crazier than you."

PK called from across the room. "We hear this all the time. Come in here with your flowery words. *Repent . . . love your neighbor . . .* And when you leave, nothin's changed."

I had no answer. Apparently, neither did Yeshua.

Tag gave a loud stretch and rose to his feet. "I believe I've heard enough for one day."

Hatch nodded and followed suit, muttering, "Class over."

I turned to see PK and Anointed also rising. For the first time since we'd begun, the two gangs found something to agree upon. (I suppose you could call that progress.)

And me? I was looking forward to having some strong words with Yeshua.

CHAPTER
TEN

IT WAS EARLY Saturday morning. The tide was higher than normal and lapping against the logs of bleached-out driftwood. The sun had barely risen but already the air was warm and humid as Siggy and I took a much-needed walk. Earlier, I tried working on my book but my mind was too scattered, a collision of thoughts and O.C. worries. I tried convincing Cindy to join us, but she was too weak—and rising before 10:00 a.m. was never her strong suit.

So it was just Siggy and me—Siggy darting over the driftwood, across the sand and chasing gulls. Me trying to make sense out of . . . *any*thing. We passed my old rowboat, usually stranded with bits of dried kelp, but thanks to the tide, it bobbed with its hull scraping against the coarse sand. There was a time on warm weekends like this when Cindy and I would take it out and just drift in the channel—Cindy reading her latest Danielle Steel, me my Walt Whitman. Or at night, looking up at the stars or down at the water, the phosphorescent glittering like bluegreen confetti.

Just up the beach, jutting from an undergrowth of holly, and shaded by a couple weathered firs, was the large, flat boulder where we shared several picnic lunches (and when the beach was deserted, more than one romantic interlude).

I can't tell you when the arguments began. Over silly things. At least I thought them silly. Some tiny lapses of thoughtfulness. Misreading her moods. Her increasing frustration with anything and everything I did or didn't do. But when you boiled it all down, I think it was mostly her boredom.

"It's like living in a prison," she complained. "There's a whole world out there and you're just content to, to . . ."

"To what?" I countered. "To provide a decent life? Carve out some stability in these crazy times?"

"To always play it safe!"

Of course, I wanted to play it safe. After my childhood—a.k.a. fieldtrip through hell—I wanted to make certain our children had everything I didn't. And they might have—were it not for our struggle to conceive. And, when we finally succeeded, the miscarriages.

It was the second that did us in.

I remember her sobbing, refusing to come out of the bedroom for days. Of course, I didn't help, clumsily saying the wrong thing at the wrong time. Gradually our walks on the beach became a thing of the past. Sex an obligation, then a memory. Our conversations turned into strained politeness. Incrementally, day by day, we stopped being husband and wife and became roommates living separate lives.

Back on the beach I watched Siggy leap and splash in his crazy attempts to catch birds he knew he could never catch. Good ol' Siggy. Despite all the insanity, he was the one thing that never changed—always faithful, a true north amidst my spinning compass.

As we walked, my mind for the hundredth time returned to yesterday's class. What had happened? How had I wound up doing another Billy Graham? It certainly wasn't planned. I hated it when people broadsided me with their religion. Give me a tract and it found its way to the nearest garbage can. But the words leaped from my mouth before I could stop them. And not some mindless Christian platitude. I really meant them. But . . . *God is love*? I actually said that? What was next, plastering my car with bumper stickers?

But I couldn't stop. Even after class. As the men filed out of the library, Sparky had lagged behind and came up to me. "You really believe that stuff," he said. "I can tell."

"Sounds strange, but I really do." And, unable to keep my mouth shut, I added, "He loves you, Sparky. Never forget that. He loves you more than he loved his own life."

But instead of laughing, or challenging me like the others, he dropped his eyes to the floor.

And, still, I couldn't keep quiet. "You know what else? He loves you more than you love yourself."

"They like me," he said. "Everyone here. They really do."

"And what about you, Sparky? Do you like you?"

He looked up to me. "You think I'm going to hell?"

"I think he loves and respects you more than you do."

He nodded, thinking. "*Imago Dei*."

"Created in his image, that's right. That's who you are. And the sooner you see yourself as he does, the sooner you'll be free."

"Free?"

I tapped my chest. "In here."

He chewed on the thought then gave a half-smile. "PK's right, you know."

"About?"

"Words are cheap. People come round here all the time saying, Jesus loves you, he died for your sins, blah, blah, blah. No offense, it's just, we hear it all the time."

I nodded, realizing I was probably no different from the others.

He took a deep breath then said, "My daddy was a minister."

"Your dad?"

"Growing up, I must've gone down that aisle a hundred times. Even went to Bible college. For a while."

"I bet he was proud."

"He left us long before any of that."

I had no words; I'd finally run out of sermon.

Sparky saved me the trouble. "Anyway, like I said, I know you mean well. Just don't get too discouraged." He turned and started for the door. "See you Monday."

"You'll be back?" I called.

He shot a look over his shoulder and grinned. "It's either you or breakfast duty."

"It's that bad?"

"Worse."

My mind kept churning throughout the morning and on into the afternoon. Not only over the impromptu revival service with the men, or my one-on-one with Sparky, but even more so with the dressing down Tag gave me—and Yeshua's insistence I not only remain silent, but ask for forgiveness.

Forgiveness? *Forgiveness?!*

I was returning from the supermarket with what amounted to a semi-truck full of food Darlene insisted we needed for tomorrow's big meal—"Hey" she said, "I make it, you pay for it"—when I heard the A/C in my car being adjusted. I glanced over and saw Yeshua in the passenger seat, vintage robe and sandals, redirecting the vent in his direction.

"You don't mind, do you?" he asked.

"Glad to share," I said.

He sat back with a contented sigh. "Sure could have used this back in my day."

"You could have come any time you wanted, right?"

He closed his eyes, enjoying the cool air against his face.

I continued, "If you would've come today, you'd have reached lots more people and a lot faster. YouTube, Twitter, Facebook—with your miracles, you'd go viral in hours."

"Not really my style."

"Right. You're more of a one-on-one kinda God."

He smiled.

"Who likes fighting with one hand tied behind your back."

Shooting me his trademark twinkle he said, "Or, with some friends, both hands."

I let out a long breath in agreement.

"Besides," he added, "the Holy Spirit has coverage the internet can't possible reach."

"Sure could have used his help at the prison yesterday."

"Who says you didn't?"

"You were there, you saw me. Not exactly a hit."

"The wind blows where it will and no one knows its coming or going."

"You're saying he was at work?"

Yeshua chuckled. "He's always at work. Can never leave well enough alone. Especially when it comes to the human heart."

"Well, he certainly did something to mine, I'll give you that."

"How so?"

"The way I broadsided the men with the gospel. And the whole race issue. You got me sounding like I was a big uh, you know . . ." I couldn't say the word.

He saved me the trouble. "You're not a racist, Will. You're just affluent. And ignorant."

I winced, not sure it was much of a concession. "So, you're on board with the whole Critical Race Theory?"

"I'm not much interested in theories. Or political issues for that matter."

"You sure? Because we've got a boatload of them."

"It's impossible to legislate the heart."

I glanced at him.

"I've come to cure the disease, not the symptoms."

"An inside job," I said. "Back to your diagram with the circles and arrows."

He nodded, "But they have to be willing. They have to ask." Turning to me, he added, "And someone has to tell them."

"Enter Will Thomas," I sighed.

He smiled and looked out the window.

Still needing to justify myself, I said, "It's just . . . my generation, we worked so hard at *not* seeing color. Like I told Tag, we took Martin Luther King's 'I Have a Dream' seriously."

Yeshua nodded. "Great speech—except that part. Talk about boring."

"Boring?"

"No one asked you to ignore color. We want you to celebrate it."

"Celebrate?"

The word barely left my mouth before we were outside, standing in a first-century street teeming with people—everyone talking, shouting, laughing. They'd gathered into large clusters, each surrounding one of Yeshua's followers.

"What's going on?" I called.

He continued to watch, his face beaming. "Check them out!" he shouted. "Go listen."

I nodded and worked my way into the nearest group. Unlike the others I'd seen in the past, these men were dressed in white muslin. Several wore gold bracelets, necklaces, a few even sported purple and blue eye shadow. In the center was the fellow I'd come to know as Thomas. But instead of sullen and sulky, he was animated, gesturing to heaven—and speaking in a language I'd never heard. Those around him listened in amazement. And when they could squeeze in a word, they asked questions—again in a language I didn't recognize.

Yeshua moved to an adjacent group which was equally enthusiastic. Their dress was closer to his, though their skin was a rich, dark ebony. In the center stood another of his disciples chattering away with the same excitement as Thomas—talking, laughing, and answering questions—in an entirely different language.

Yeshua looked over to me and shouted, "Now this is what I call a party!"

I moved from my crowd to his. Because of the different languages, I took a wild guess. "Is this Pentecost?"

He grinned, motioning to all the groups. "Like I said, it's hard to hold the Holy Spirit back! Do you see any racism here? Anyone threatened or being threatened?"

I looked about. Of the dozen groups surrounding us, each bubbled with enthusiasm and joy.

"They're from different tribes and countries," he shouted. "Not one color—but a mosaic of colors—every one created to enrich the other."

"It's quite a show."

"A celebration!" Yeshua corrected. "And exactly what we intended."

"So, what happened?" I shouted. "Why all the division?"

Suddenly we were back in my car, everything strangely quiet—and, by contrast, a bit sad.

I regained my bearings, adjusted the sun visor. "Why did all that stop?"

"For some, it never has. But with others . . ." He looked back out the window.

"With others?" I questioned.

His answer was soft. "Fear."

"Fear?"

"The same fear you and Pete felt trying to walk on the water."

"Racism is fear?"

He said nothing.

"So, is there a way to beat it?"

Even more softly, he replied, "No."

"No? Are you telling me racism will just keep on—"

"You can't beat it, Will. You can only replace it."

"Replace it? With . . .?"

"With what you felt yesterday when you went toe-to-toe with men who could have easily hurt you."

I shook my head. "Honestly, I still don't know what came over me."

"Love."

His answer was too easy. A bromide. "I'm sorry," I said. "How can I love a guy like that?"

"Not your love. Mine."

I frowned.

"You can't love him, Will. Not on your own. But you trusted me enough, you let me inside enough to change you, to let my love push out your fear."

"So—we're back to your diagram again."

"We're back to the Holy Spirit. Changing you from the inside. Spilling out, soaking others.

I slowly quoted, "*Rivers of living water.*"

"Exactly."

I paused then argued, "But you saw his response. I had zero impact."

"Zero impact?"

"Other than sounding like a walking cliché."

"Answer your phone."

"What? My phone isn't—"

My cell rang. I gave Yeshua a look and dug it out of my pocket. "Hello?"

"Doc? This is Assistant Warden Stamph."

"Hello, Warden. What—"

"We had an incident."

"An incident?"

"Jonathan DeSoto.

"Who?"

"Sparky. He's in the infirmary. Been askin' for you."

"Me? What happened? Is he all right?"

"It's late, but if you come by, I can arrange a visit."

"Now? This afternoon?"

I turned to Yeshua, but the passenger seat was empty.

PART TWO

ELEVEN

"IT'S BEEN A long day," Assistant Warden Stamph said as he slid open the heavy metal door to the prison infirmary. "I'm headin' home, but you're in good hands with the doctor here."

A graying, middle-aged woman with sturdy legs rose from her desk.

"Dr. Collins," Stamph said, "meet Professor Thomas."

She extended her hand and we shook. "I've heard a lot about you," she said.

I wasn't exactly sure what that meant. Stamph's explanation didn't help. "She's one of you."

"One of . . ."

"Christian," he said.

"Oh. Okay . . ."

"Take care of him" were his last words before turning and stepping back into the hallway.

"Thanks . . ." I answered as he pulled the door shut with an ominous thud.

It was late, well past visiting hours. Why Stamph not only allowed me on the grounds, but for the second time in three days, personally greeted and ushered me through security was a mystery.

As if reading my mind, the doctor explained, "He's a good man. Really cares about the inmates."

"I'm guessing this isn't protocol."

She was careful to avoid an answer.

"He won't get busted, will he?"

"The staff's a tight community." She motioned toward the beds. "Shall we?"

I nodded and we started down the long, narrow room lit by bare fluorescents. To my left, rose a wall, the top-half painted white, the bottom-half military green. Along the top were a handful of opaque, wire-meshed windows. To my right, a dozen hospital beds; only three curtained off with what I guessed to be patients.

"So you're the infamous Preacher Man," she said.

"Actually, I'm not a—did you say *infamous*?"

"Like I said, we're pretty tight."

I still wasn't certain what she meant and before I could ask we came to a stop at one of the curtained-off beds. She pulled aside the cloth, more bedsheet than curtain, and there he lay sleeping under a thin blanket. The room was spartan—bed, IV stand, and some basic monitoring equipment. Beside the bed was a molded, fiberglass chair.

"What exactly happened?" I asked.

"Stamph didn't tell you?"

"Just that he got in some fight. Said you'd explain the details."

"Guess the little guy took what you said to heart."

"About?"

"Hernandez is the Latino shot caller. Runs most of the compound. He summoned Sparky for a booty call. And the kid here, he had the audacity to say no."

I frowned. "Because . . . of what I said?"

"He has a reputation for being, what we say, sexually fluid—depending upon the wishes of his clientele.

"And?"

"Hernandez expressed his wishes. Sparky refused. Hernandez repeated. Sparky dug in. And Hernandez communicated his displeasure by assuring the kid would be less fluid. Permanently."

"I don't understand."

"They cut him up pretty bad down there."

I turned to Sparky, a sick realization taking hold. Had he actually put into practice what I said? Stood up for what was right? And . . . was I responsible?

Motioning to the chair, the doctor said, "Stay as long as you like."

I simply nodded.

"He's heavily sedated. To ease the pain."

"It's . . ." I cleared my throat, "it's pretty bad?"

"He won't be having children, if that's what you mean."

I could only stare down at him.

"Well, I'll be up at my desk in case you need anything."

I nodded, heard her exit as she pulled the curtain shut.

"What have I done?" I whispered, more in prayer than to him. I eased myself down into the chair. As if sensing my presence, Sparky rolled his head toward me, then slowly opened a swollen eye.

"Hey there," I said huskily.

He continued to stare.

"It's me. Dr. Thomas. Preacher Man."

With a groan, full of as much pain as disgust, he turned his head away.

Alright, I deserved that.

I tried again. "Sounds like you stood up to that Hernandez character."

No response.

"Maybe . . ." I cleared my throat again. "They said you asked for me."

There was no answer. Only the buzz of the overhead fluorescents.

CHAPTER
TWELVE

SITTING THERE, STARING at Sparky's back, I couldn't help but wonder what all he'd seen and been through. Not just here in prison, but before. Like all of us, he'd started out as a baby, God's precious child. A blank slate full of possibility. Then what? What dug into his soul, scarring it so deeply he felt compelled to go down his father's church aisle time after time hoping God would forgive him? What happened inside him when that same father abandoned them? And why Bible college after that? Searching for truth? Still striving for approval? Was he so starved for affection—"they really like me"—that he'd subject himself to acts I can't even imagine?

I stared at his back—fragile shoulders that reminded me of Cindy's that first night she came home. Both of them so vulnerable, so lost. *Imago Dei.* How we beat and batter that image until it's barely visible. I thought of Darlene. The little girl sexually molested by her deacon uncle. Her demands for a teenage daughter's abortion that left both daughter and unborn grandbaby dead. Amber with her absentee mom. Me and my dad. Even Patricia with her protective, religious armor. All of us starting off in his image until the crippling began. A crippling that, despite all the wounds, all the infection, all the decay, could never quite extinguish his presence. All my life I'd been quick to compile and categorize people's failures. But now labels were falling away. I began seeing the glimmer, sometimes impossibly faint, of God's image inside each of us—underneath all the failures and debilitating fear. What was it Yeshua said, back in his home town? *"I have come to set the prisoners free?"* Without even knowing it, I'd begun seeing people as prisoners struggling to break out of their chains. *"Not enemies,"* he had said. *"But prisoners of war."*

And he said something else, equally radical: *"I don't see what's wrong with people. I see what's missing."*

How long I sat there staring at Sparky, I'm not sure— my mind alternating between Yeshua's words and my own guilt. Was the boy here because of me, because of what I said? Was I another authority figure he was trying to earn approval from? I don't remember dozing off. But I do remember being startled awake by shouting voices.

I glanced to Sparky who remained asleep. Rising, I turned and drew the curtain aside and was blinded by bright, afternoon sunshine. As my eyes adjusted, I recognized the brilliant white walls of Jerusalem's temple about fifty feet away. In front of me was a large plaza where two dozen men stood, firing questions at Yeshua, their tone anything but friendly.

I threw a quick look to Sparky, then stepped through the curtain and onto the plaza.

"If I'm telling you the truth," Yeshua was saying, "why won't you believe me? I'll say it again. Whoever belongs to God hears God. It's as simple as that. If you don't hear, you don't belong."

"The man's a Samaritan!" someone in the crowd shouted.

"Demon-possessed!" another yelled.

Shading my eyes against the sun, I noticed some of Yeshua's disciples distancing themselves from him—taking one or two steps backward. Or three.

"I'm not demon-possessed," Yeshua said. "What I am is honoring my Father. And what you're doing is dishonoring me." This did not exactly calm the crowd. He continued, "I'm not seeking my own glory, but there is someone who wants to reveal it—and he, my friends, is your judge."

"You dare tell us God is glorifying you!" It was a big, hulking man. Put him in tan pants with matching coat and he'd fit in with my incarcerated friends.

Jesus answered. "What I am saying, and listen to me; whoever obeys the words I'm speaking will never see death."

"Now we *know* you're demon-possessed!" the man shouted.

Another yelled, "Abraham died and so did all the prophets, and you say whoever obeys you won't die?"

"Who do you think you are?" another cried from the back. "Are you greater than our father, Abraham?"

"He died!" the big man shouted.

"So did the prophets!" another yelled.

Yeshua raised his voice to be heard. "If I glorify myself, my glory means nothing. But my Father, who you claim is your God, he is the one glorifying me!" Ignoring my past advice to brush up on his people skills, he continued. "There is absolutely no way you know him. But I do. If I said I didn't, I would be a liar like you!"

They roared in fury.

"I know him and I obey his word!" Shouting over them, he continued, "Your father Abraham was thrilled at the thought of seeing my day. And he saw it and he was glad!"

"You're not fifty years old!" the big man yelled, his face turning crimson, "And you've seen Abraham?"

Without missing a beat, Yeshua answered, "Listen to me! Listen to me carefully!" He waited as they settled. "Are you listening?" When he had their attention he quietly replied, "Before Abraham was . . . I Am."

The crowd went crazy. "Stone him!" they shouted. "Kill the blasphemer! Kill him!" Several stooped, searching for rocks.

Having made his point, Yeshua figured it might be a good time to leave. He turned and started off; not running, but not exactly strolling either.

That's when he spotted me. "What say, Will?" he called. "Good time for an exit?"

I nodded and joined him as we headed into the nearest alley, the men not far behind, continuing their meltdown.

As we picked up our pace, I said, "You sure know how to inspire a crowd."

We turned right and jogged down another alley—the shade of the buildings a welcomed relief from the plaza's heat.

"Truth isn't always popular," he said. "It can be enough to get a God killed."

I shot him a look. If that was humor, neither of us laughed. We turned into a third alley. The voices behind us, gradually faded. Since I was running out of breath, Yeshua motioned for us to slow down and stop. I gave no argument.

"We'll be okay here?" I asked, leaning over to catch my breath.

He nodded and after a moment asked, "So, how's it going with you?"

"You saw what they did to Sparky?"

He looked down and sadly nodded.

"So why?" I asked. "The kid was trying to do the right thing."

"Yes."

"Yes?" I repeated. I straightened up. "That's no answer."

"Yes, he resisted evil. And, yes, he stood up for truth."

"And that's his reward?"

Fixing his eyes on me, Yeshua asked, "What would you like it to be?"

"I don't know. How 'bout a little protection? Maybe some of the peace and joy you're always talking about? *I came to give life and give it abundantly.* Isn't that one of your mottos?"

"It is. And he'll have it."

I looked away, biting my tongue.

But, as was his habit, he wouldn't let it go. "What?" he said.

I shook my head, knowing I'd shot my mouth off too many times.

"Talk to me, Will."

I hesitated.

"Come on, I know what you're thinking anyway."

"Okay, alright." I took a breath and began. "You promise peace, and joy, and protection?"

"Yes, I do."

"After what happened to Sparky, I wouldn't exactly call that truth in advertising, would you?"

He paused, then quietly answered. "I never promised to take you around hard times. I promised to give you peace and joy as you go *through* them."

"The balloon metaphor, I get it. Your presence inside pushing against outside circumstances."

"*In this world you will have tribulation.* That's another one of my promises. *But be of good cheer, I've overcome the world.*"

I blew out my breath in frustration.

"Will, nearly all of my disciples will be murdered. Other followers will have their families tortured and killed in front of them—not to mention facing an ongoing stream of deceit, lies, and bigotry. But when it's over, each and every one will count it a privilege."

"In heaven, I get it. But what about the here and now?"

"As I said . . . Tribulation. Affliction."

"That's *not* the Christianity people are selling."

"Which may be why so many have turned their backs on me. They've bought the wrong bill of goods."

I could only stare.

"I don't know how I can make it any clearer." He paused then continued. "At this very moment in your world, in your time, fifteen of my brothers and sisters are murdered every day for following me."

"Fifteen!" I said. "Every day?"

"That's nearly 5,500 killed each year."

"For being Christian!?"

He nodded. Then he took a breath and solemnly quoted, "*No servant is greater than his master. If they persecute me, they'll persecute you.*" He closed his eyes. I could only watch as he continued. *"Blessed are you when people hate you—when they exclude you—when they insult you—and when they reject your name as evil because of the Son of Man."*

He slowly reopened them and looked directly at me. *"Rejoice in that day and leap for joy, because great is your reward in heaven."*

THIRTEEN

"PREACHER?"

I felt a hand on my shoulder and woke with a start. Blinking, I managed to focus on Sparky still asleep on the bed before me. While above, stood another man—black, early thirties, buzz-cut, and wearing inmate clothes.

"Sorry to wake you."

"No, I, uh . . . what time is it?"

"Doc says we should clear you out before shift change."

"Right," I said, giving my eyes a swipe.

He reached for my arm. "Need any help?"

"No, I'm good," I said as I stiffly rose to my feet.

He stepped aside to let me pass through the open curtain. No first-century buildings on the other side. Just the long room, with beds to my left, and to the right, wire-meshed windows filled with morning light. As we walked, I pulled out my cell to check the time.

6:42 a.m.! What?

We approached Dr. Collins's desk and she looked up from her paperwork to smile. "Good morning."

"I'm sorry," I said, "I must have fallen asleep."

"No worries." She rose. "But we should get you on your way." She nodded to my escort. "Miller, here, will see you out."

I nodded as he crossed to the heavy green door and pulled it open. "Right this way, sir."

I turned back to Collins, not exactly sure what to say. "Well . . . thank you."

"No, Professor," she said, reaching out her hand, "thank *you*."

As we shook I said, "I'm afraid I didn't do much. When he wasn't sleeping, apparently, I was."

She gave an amused nod. "I'm sure you helped; just showing up. What does the Lord say? Whatever you do for the least of his you do for him?"

I appreciated the encouragement but knew better. Doing nothing, despite intentions, still amounted to nothing. Or so I thought.

"Preacher?" Miller motioned to the open door.

I turned and joined him. As we entered the hall and he began pulling the door shut, the doctor called, "Miller?"

He paused. "Yes ma'am."

"Be sure to take the scenic route."

They shared a faint smile. "Yes ma'am."

We started down the long corridor. Miller's pace was young and spry. Mine was old and rusty, still working out the kinks from last night's sleeping arrangement.

"So, how's he doin?" he asked. "Sparky."

"The doctor has him pretty sedated."

"Yeah. Kid's got guts though, huh? Nobody says no to Hernandez. You really lit a fire under him."

"Apparently," I said, anything but enthusiastic. "At least that's what the doctor and your assistant warden said."

"Warden Stamph? He's a trip, huh? All business on the outside, tapioca inside."

"Tapioca?"

"Pudding. But the dude's on his way to becomin' the real deal."

I was struck by the phrase. "Real deal," I said. "That's what he called Dr. Collins last night."

"Yeah."

"Which is what—being a Christian?"

"More like a follower of Jesus. You know, the real ones."

"I didn't know there was a difference."

He snickered, like I'd made a joke.

We came to another hallway. But instead of turning left, as I had with Stamph, we turned right.

"Where are we going?" I pointed left. "That's how I came in last night."

"Doc said the scenic route."

"You're going to show more of the prison to me?"

"Nah."

"Then . . ."

"I'm going to show more of you to the prison."

"Excuse me?"

"It's cool, man. It's cool."

I waited for more. But when it appeared that was all the intel I was getting, I circled back to our discussion. "So, are there many of you here? The 'real deals'?"

"Yeah. A place like this really helps a guy get his—" he did a quick verbal edit, "—act together."

"I bet it does."

"Everyone knows the talk. We hear it all the time. But only a few walk the walk."

"'The real deals,'" I repeated.

"We stick close. Watch each other's back. Have to in a place like this."

"Lots of harassment?"

"Nah. Nobody gets beat or shanked or nothin' like that. Small change stuff—cut from groups, a little trash talk. Course there's always some dude testing you, tryin' to take advantage 'cause he thinks you soft."

I nodded. He could just as easily been talking about my own home.

He pushed open a side door and we stepped out into a morning drizzle. It was a small courtyard, nothing like their large, exercise yard. Twenty feet to my left a line of inmates stood waiting at the door of another building. Heads turned toward us. All two dozen of them. They kept their stares blank, but there was no missing their curiosity. My gate stiffened. I looked down to examine the tufts of grass at my feet.

"You doin' okay?" Miller asked.

"Yeah."

"They're in line for breakfast. Most important meal of the day. If you can keep it down."

"Hey, Preacher Man."

I looked up and saw Tag near the front of the line. He gave a nod, a summon for us to join him.

Miller swore under his breath.

I lowered my voice. "Should we keep walking?"

"Too late, now." Miller glanced to both sides then started toward him. "C'mon."

I hesitated, searching for guards. None were in sight. I had two choices; stand by myself under the gaze of two dozen hardened convicts or . . .

I joined Miller. As we approached, Hatchet and a man I didn't recognize stepped forward to block us. If Yeshua was around, now would be as good a time as any for another visit.

Tag motioned to me. "Just him."

Miller nodded. I hesitated.

"C'mon," Hatch said, "breakfast is waiting."

I stepped forward; grateful I still had some control over my legs.

"What are you doing here?" Tag said.

"I, uh," I cleared my throat and managed to get out another word. "Sparky."

"You here checking on him?"

"Yes." I did another quick survey of the courtyard. No guards. No Yeshua.

Tag nodded. "Yeah, pretty messed up what they did to him."

"Hernandez?" I said.

Tag signaled me to lower my voice. "No worries," he said. "We'll be taking care of it. 'Vengeance is mine, saith the Lord,' right?" He gave a smile. If it was to comfort me, it didn't succeed. "And we're going to give him a helping hand. Soon." I searched his face and he nodded. "Real soon."

"Okay, girls," a voice shouted from a door opening at the front of the line. "Let's move."

The line started forward. Tag motioned for my dismissal and I stepped back to join Miller.

We resumed our trek across the courtyard. Arriving at another door, we stepped into a hallway that looked more familiar to me. Up ahead and to the right was the bullet-proof, glass-enclosed guard room where two guards watched rows of monitors. As we approached, Miller nodded to one of them who punched a button. The first door unlocked with a loud buzz.

As it slid open I turned back to Miller and thanked him.

"No sir," he said. "Thank *you*."

I gave a nod, for what I wasn't sure, and stepped forward. The door shut behind me and another in front buzzed open. A moment later, I walked into the lobby and my freedom . . . or so I thought.

CHAPTER

FOURTEEN

"LONG NIGHT?" YESHUA'S comment was more observation than question as we walked across the prison parking lot.

My mind was going a hundred directions at once and I wasn't sure what to say. I was tired, cranky, and more than a little confused.

"Talk to me, Will."

I wanted to demand what crazy and absurd "adventure" he was taking me on this time. But somehow I managed to stay quiet and keep my thoughts to myself. (And we all know how well that works, right?)

Suddenly we were back in the hot sun of the Middle East. Beside us was a large lake. Only it wasn't Galilee. To our left rose brown hills and dirt cliffs. And across the water, some ten miles or so, it was the same. Everything was brown. Nothing resembled anything green.

"What is this place?" I asked.

He motioned to the waves lapping the shore. "This is the same water you saw me baptized in."

I shook my head. "No. You were baptized in the Jordan River. Everything there was lush, and green and . . ."

"Alive?"

"Yeah, alive." I scanned the barren hills and shore. "Everything here is dead."

"Hence, the name."

"Hence the—" I stopped. "Is this the Dead Sea?"

He nodded. "And yet it's the same water. It started up in Galilee with its green hills, its people, its lake full of fish. Then it flowed down the Jordan, also full of life, until it finally arrived here."

"Where it became dead?"

Again he nodded.

"But why?" I asked. "How?"

"It has no outlet here. Instead of giving up its water like the Galilee, or the Jordan, it hordes it. There's no place for it to go so it just sits in the hot sun and evaporates; leaving behind all its salts and minerals which continue to build and build until it's toxic. The very water that was supposed to give life, now kills it."

I looked out over the lake. "And you're showing me this because . . ."

"It's the same water. The difference is what you do with it. Do you give it up to have life? Or cling to it and die."

I slowly nodded.

"You can't outgive us, Will. *Give and it will be given to you. A good measure, pressed down, shaken together, and running over.* The more of your life you pour into others, the more of our life we pour into you. Life, that's what I'm about. Abundant, overflowing."

"Compared to this," I said, motioning to the water.

He closed his eyes and quietly quoted, *"Depart from me, you who are cursed, into the eternal fire prepared for the devil and his angels. For I was hungry and you gave me nothing to eat, I was thirsty and you gave me nothing to drink, I was a stranger and you did not invite me in, I needed clothes and you did not clothe me, I was sick and in prison and you did not look after me."*

Opening his eyes, he turned to me. "My love cuts both ways, Will. There's truth. But there's also grace. One sword, two edges."

And then I was back in the parking lot. By myself.

I unlocked the car and climbed in—his words still lingering in my head. A double-edged sword. How does that apply to Sparky? Had I used the wrong edge, wielding too much truth by calling him out? If I hadn't, he'd be well and unharmed. And what about Cindy? Was I being too soft? Enabling her, as Patricia said?

You can hear the sound of the wind, but you can't tell where it comes from or where it's going. So it is with everyone born of the Spirit. Well, he was right about that. When it came to coming or going I hadn't a clue. But he was also right about something else . . . Like that crazy diagram he drew, I was changing. It was slow and definitely painful, but I was changing.

I pulled from the parking lot and turned onto the main road when my cell rang. Darlene, according to caller ID.

I picked up and answered, "Hey there."

"Good morning, slugger. She still there?"

"She? Oh, you mean . . . well, I—"

"Let me guess. You still haven't confronted her."

"Long story."

"You really need to grow a pair of testosterone producers?"

"I see you're cleaning up your language."

"Practicing my church-speech."

"Your church—" Then it hit me. This was Sunday morning. The day we were all going to church . . . Patricia, Darlene and me.

"So tell me," she said, "what does one wear to archaic rituals these days?"

I glanced down at my rumpled shirt and pants, realizing I had no time to go home for a shower or change. "Actually," I said, "dress is pretty casual." Then, realizing how provocatively Darlene defined casual, I added, "What you wear to class would be good. Lots of kids from school will be there."

She swore. "Just what I need—the college thinking I got religion. You know I'm not crazy about this?"

"I figured."

"But a deal's a deal. If it's the only way to get the squatter out of your house, I'll take one for the team. But you, you wait outside for me. Don't make me go in there by myself."

"Okay."

"Service is at 11:00 so catch an early ferry, just in case."

"Right," I said, not bothering to explain where I spent the night.

"Don't make me stand around."

I glanced at my watch. "I'll be plenty early."

"Don't be late."

"Trust me."

"I mean it. Be there."

"See you soon."

"You better."

We hung up and I quietly mused. In all the time I've known Darlene, I'd never heard her quite so nervous.

FIFTEEN

STANDING IN THE lobby of the coffee house, Darlene motioned to the restrooms. "Is she ever going to come out of there?"

"Hi, Dr. Pratford, a passing goth said. Her girlfriend added, "Nice to see you, Doctor."

Darlene nodded, "Ladies." Turning back to me, she whispered, "She's doing this on purpose, you know."

"On purpose?"

"Making me a spectacle."

"I really don't think that's Patricia's style."

"And suddenly you're an expert on women?"

She had me there. I may be surrounded by them—babies to teens to exes to Patricia and Darlene—but my understanding of the female mind had not improved. On the contrary, it only seemed to get worse.

"Sup, Doctor?" A geeky student with two buddies passed, all three in flip-flops and cargo pants.

She nodded and smiled.

"Doctor." A beautiful co-ed passed, arm intwined with a corresponding football type.

Another nod, another smile. Then to me, "How come no one greets you?" Before I replied she answered. "Still persona non grata?"

"Let's just say—"

"I suppose defending sexual predators will do that."

Of course, she was referring to the recent debacle of standing up for my friend—which you may remember cost both my job and reputation. It happened several weeks ago, but the rush to judgment was still very much present.

"There she is now," Darlene said.

Patricia moved through the crowd, looking as stunning as ever in a beige, crocheted dress and forest-green shawl. "Are we ready?" she asked as she arrived.

"For the past ten minutes," Darlene said.

Patricia managed a polite smile. "Then we should find a seat."

She turned and led us into the coffee shop, a converted warehouse teeming with college kids who milled about or sat at small round tables. The walls were illuminated by a handful of floor lights. The rest of the room was lit by candles, one per table. The smell of freshly ground coffee filled the air.

Patricia moved through the room, passing so many empty tables that Darlene finally called out, "Where are you taking us?"

Pretending not to hear, she continued leading us toward the front of the room. Students looked up and smiled. Many recognized Darlene. One or two even gave Patricia a thumbs-up.

"Did you see that?" Darlene fumed. "She's treating me like a trophy."

We eventually landed at a front table—just two over from the pastor, Dr. Stewart, a stately looking black man who I enjoyed listening to in the past.

"Really?" Darlene said.

Patricia smiled and offered her a chair. "Best seat in the house."

The two exchanged looks I didn't quite understand and common sense told me not to pry. But if the refined and genteel Patricia Swenson thought she was putting Darlene on the spot, well I'm afraid she didn't know who she was up against.

We took our seats, Darlene on my left, Patricia on my right. Flagging down one of the volunteer servers, Darlene ordered coffee and offered to buy ours. Patricia declined. After my all-nighter at the prison, I asked for a double. Just as the server turned to leave, I noticed Patricia stiffen.

"Something wrong?" I asked.

"What's he doing here?" she whispered.

"Who?"

She motioned to a pleasant-looking gentleman sitting beside Stewart and his wife. His blonde hair and beard were neatly trimmed and he wore a white vest with matching shirt and jacket. Glasses hung from a beaded strap around his neck.

She continued, "He's the minister of that gay church down in Mount Vernon."

Darlene leaned forward. "What's up?" she asked.

"That man," Patricia whispered. "He's gay."

"Oh, no," Darlene turned to stare—and loud enough to be heard by their table, she said, "He's a queer?"

Stewart, wife, and their guest turned toward us.

Patricia looked down. But for Darlene Pratford, it was payback time. "Glory to God, Sis! Maybe he'll repent and vote Republican just like us!"

With bowed head Patricia still managed to shoot her a death glare. Darlene blinked, feigning innocence. I didn't have the courage to check the expressions at Stewart's table.

Our coffee eventually arrived and the service started. It began with some kid on a stool with guitar leading the crowd in a couple songs everyone except Darlene and I knew. When he finished, Stewart rose, coffee cup in hand. He greeted us in his slight Jamaican accent, made a few announcements, then got down to business:

"I should like to take a break from our studies in Ephesians and today introduce to you a friend who is very dear. Jay Charles York was the first to reach out to Margot and myself when we lost our daughter to suicide nine years ago this month. We quickly became friends and to this day share a lunch or two each year."

"More often if you'd ever pick up the tab," York called.

Light chuckles filled the room.

Stewart continued, "He is the senior pastor at Grace Brethren in Mount Vernon. A church ministering primarily to our LGBTQ community."

Darlene beamed over at Patricia who watched, drained of expression.

"Now Reverend York is not welcomed in several Christian circles, which I understand. But as a man who struggles with same-sex attraction all of his life, he is able to reach out and touch others in a way I never can."

Darlene leaned to Patricia and whispered, "I bet he can, the nasty little degenerate."

It was my turn to shoot Darlene a glare. She gave a shrug and nodded, realizing she'd gone too far, even by her standards.

Stewart continued, "We do not always agree, but this I must tell you, the man loves Jesus as much as, perhaps even more than I. And it is for that reason, I have asked him to come share with us this morning."

Patricia reached for her purse.

"What are you doing?" I whispered.

She shook her head, making it clear she was leaving.

"Please," I said, setting my hand on her arm, "stay."

She hesitated, saw my sincerity along with my subtle motion to Darlene. Against her better judgment, she sat back and waited.

Stewart continued, "So, join me, if you would, in welcoming Reverend Jay Charles York."

As the crowd clapped, some hooting, Patricia whispered, "I can't believe he invited that man to share the pulpit."

I glanced back to Darlene who watched with interest as the two ministers exchanged hugs and York took his place behind the rickety lectern. Keeping an eye each on Patricia and Darlene, I listened—all the time wondering what direction the Wind was blowing this time.

York began. "Your pastor is right. When it comes to LGBTQ the two of us land on entirely opposite sides of the issue."

"Preach it, brother," Stewart called.

York chuckled. "But the reason I'm standing before you today, and the reason your pastor is speaking to my church later next month, is because, for us, it's not an issue."

Patricia fidgeted, liking that statement even less.

"I'm serious," York said. "We are not talking an issue here. For us it is not an abstract argument, a political position, or even a theological debate. For us, it's people. Individuals. Like you. Like me. Each created in God's image."

Again, with the imago Dei, I thought. Somebody's sure trying to make a point.

He continued, "Children of a loving Father who sees each of us with such value he was willing to sacrifice his Son to be with us. Because you see, as great as our disagreements are over Scripture—and we've had some doozies, haven't we, Pastor?"

"Amen," Stewart laughed.

York gave another chuckle. "But as great as those disagreements may be, the two of us realize that even if we get the Bible right, but get our love wrong, we're still . . . wrong."

Patricia had reached her limit. Once again, she clutched her purse preparing to leave. And this time no pleading or puppy dog eyes on my part could convince her to stay.

He continued, "I'm not suggesting some feel-good panacea—or an excuse to discard any pursuit of holiness. And I'm certainly not here to convince you of my position. No. I'm only here so you see me. And I see you. I mean *really* see." He paused making sure he had the room's full attention before opening his Bible. Let me read something to you from 1 Corinthians 6:9–10. Because if you believe these verses apply to today, you and I may be less different than you think."

As the crowd opened their own Bibles (mostly phone apps), Patricia took advantage of the moment to rise. And, as difficult as I knew it was for her, as several eyes turned to watch, she started for the exit.

I was unsure what to do. Follow her? Be her escort? Provide the strength and support I could tell she needed?

Darlene didn't help. "See you at the cross burnings, Sis!"

"Come on," I growled.

Darlene simply shook her head.

By the time I turned back to Patricia, she was halfway through the room. And still I sat. Conflicted? Yes. Cowardly? Absolutely. Unsure what to believe, and hating myself, anyway? All boxes checked.

And then she was gone.

Saying a little prayer for her (and recognizing even that was the chicken's way out) I reluctantly turned back to York. He'd found his place in Scripture and began to read:

"Do you not know that wrongdoers will not inherit the kingdom of God? Do not be deceived: Neither the sexually immoral—" He paused and looked up. "How many of you are having sex now, before you're married, or looking at porn, or . . . well, the list goes on, doesn't it?"

No one was in a confessional mood, but he had their attention.

Returning to the Bible, he resumed. *"Neither will idolaters*—" Again he looked up. "Anybody here dwell on your grades, or looks, or social status, more than God?"

When there was no response, he continued reading, "*Nor adulterers.*" Looking up again, he asked, "Know anybody divorced who's thinking it's okay to re-marry?"

He returned to the verses. "*Nor men who have sex with men.*" Still staring at the page, he silently raised his hand.

You could hear a pin drop.

He continued. "*Nor thieves, nor the greedy.* Anybody keep silent over receiving too much change? How 'bout sharing a streaming channel? *Nor drunkards.* How 'bout those Friday night parties? Whew. Hang on, we're almost finished. He turned back and read. *Nor slanderers.* I'm sure no one here ever talks trash about anyone. *Nor swindlers.* And none of us use half-truths to make the best impression or get the best deal."

He paused a long moment, then slowly closed the book. "I tell you the truth . . ." then recited the last verse by memory, "*None of these will inherit the kingdom of God.*"

If it was quiet before, the silence was now downright eerie.

He removed his glasses and looked into our faces. "You see. There's no difference. We're all in desperate need of forgiveness. Let me repeat: We all, each of us, desperately need the forgiveness of Jesus Christ." He hesitated, then added. "Though, there might be one difference. How many here have, because of your failures, been so shamed by others or so full of self-hatred that you've either tried to commit suicide or have seriously considered it?"

After a long pause, he replied. "If I were to ask that same question of my congregation, every hand would rise."

CHAPTER
SIXTEEN

THERE'S A REVERENCE when you're with someone dying. Their past offenses seem . . . less offensive. At least that's how it was with Cindy. As I knelt at the bedside, easing her boney feet covered with paper-thin skin into her sneakers, my hurt and resentment faded. Don't get me wrong, I was still cautious. If I didn't keep up some wall, I'd melt back into the emotional puddle I'd worked so hard to climb out of when she first left. But as the two of us sat in that tiny bedroom sharing memories—and there were some good ones—I felt that wall slowly eroding. Granted, she was a bit high from the marijuana, but in a strange way, even that made her more vulnerable, drawing out some need in me to protect and defend her. Something I'd rid myself of months ago . . . or so I thought.

Earlier, Darlene and I remained through the rest of the church service—though when it was over she couldn't get out of there fast enough. Patricia held true to her word (as she always does) catching an earlier ferry out to the house, meeting Cindy and subtly checking to see if the prognosis was true. By the time Darlene and I arrived, the verdict was in. My ex was, indeed, dying. Penniless. The prodigal wife returned home for her final days.

Would it be inconvenient? Of course. The house was matchbox-small, more so with Amber and the baby. But if this was where she needed to be—with the beach, the fresh ocean air, and memories—if staying here gave her any comfort in her final hours, I could make the minor adjustments—even if it meant sleeping on the sofa . . . while she slept with her boyfriend in my bed!

Okay, maybe some adjustments weren't so minor.

And now, as Darlene called everyone in for supper, a massive affair filling the house with incredible smells, I knelt in the tiny room helping Cindy into her shoes.

"You know, she's a good woman," Cindy said.

"Who's that?" I asked.

"Patricia. She's wound a bit tight, I'll give you that, but you could do a lot worse."

"Meaning?"

"Will . . ." She gave me a look making it clear even after a year's absence she knew me better than I knew myself. "She's good."

"You could tell that in one meeting?"

"She didn't treat me like some druggie or gold digger, I'll tell you that."

"Gold digger?"

"I'm no idiot. I know what everyone's thinking."

I reached for her hands. "Ready to stand?"

She nodded and I helped her to her feet—her wrists thin and frail.

"Trust me," she said. "Underneath all that cover-girl beauty, which we all hate her for, she's got a huge heart."

"And a judgmental one," I said. "You should have seen her in church this morning."

"She wasn't that way with me. She may be passionate with strong opinions, but it's a passion for doing right. You can't judge people for wanting that, can you?"

"Me, judging someone for being judgy?" We chuckled, neither of us missing the irony.

I opened the door and she leaned on me as we started down the hall, one step after another, heading toward the voices in the dining room.

"Of course," she said, "Darlene's no slouch, either."

"Darlene?" I asked in surprise.

Cindy gave a laugh that turned into coughing so violent we had to stop until she finished.

"You okay?" I asked.

She nodded and motioned us onward.

"Darlene's just a friend," I said. "Actually, she's more Amber's friend than mine. A surrogate mother."

"Sure she is."

"What's that supposed to mean?"

"It means you're going to have to make a decision, my friend. And with those two, the sooner the better."

I could have argued, but trying to convince Cindy of anything never worked when we were married and there was no reason to suspect it would start now.

"Honestly." She shook her head. "I can't leave you on your own for a few months before you have more women than you know what to do with . . ."

I hated it when she was right.

As we approached the dining room, I heard Patricia's voice—thinner and more reedy than normal—a sheer sign she was on the defense. "Zim, Zir, Zis, Zieself . . . and you poor teens, already struggling with identity. Now you have to figure this out as well?"

Amber shot back, "Who knows us better than us?"

"Yeah," Chip agreed.

"God."

Patricia's abruptness stopped them cold.

We rounded the corner as Darlene was setting a giant bowl of mashed potatoes on the table before Patricia, Amber, and of course, Chip, who always managed to drop in when there was a free meal. "So tell us, Patty," she said. "What about all the trans in this country who'd like to be treated with a modicum of respect?"

"I am not suggesting disrespect. I am merely stating that according to the CDC .03 to .08 percent of the entire population claim to be transgender." (As always Patricia was as direct as she was informed.) "And for that we are to change the English language?"

More silence.

"Ah, Cindy." Darlene spotted us. "Here," she crossed to an empty setting and pulled out the chair.

"It smells wonderful," Cindy said as I helped her to her seat.

"It tastes better than that," Darlene said. She motioned to her Southern cooking which was on full display. Fried chicken, black-eyed peas, mashed potatoes and gravy, turnip greens, sweet corn, pimento cheese on celery sticks, corn bread—along with some fried green tomatoes just to show off.

"And where do I sit?" I asked.

"Oh, right," Darlene said. "Somebody scoot over and make room for him." She turned and headed back to the kitchen. "I'll grab a plate."

SEVENTEEN

BY THE TIME we began eating, the debate had returned to full speed with Patricia leading the charge—if you can lead a charge with your back against the wall. "Every reputable historian agrees, the Bible is the most accurate ancient manuscript in the history of mankind."

"Human kind," Amber corrected.

"Most accurate or most oppressive?" An obvious intent on Darlene's part to get under Patricia's skin.

But Patricia was too sophisticated to lose her cool—although her voice still was a bit in the soprano range. "Jesus Christ was the first religious leader to elevate the status of women. His teachings led to the abolishment of slavery, not to mention erecting hospitals, universities, creating untold number of charitable organizations."

"Actually," Cindy weighed in, her voice soft and frail. "I don't think anybody's questioning the teaching of Jesus."

"If he even existed," Chip scoffed. "I mean just 'cause the Bible says something doesn't make it—"

Patricia cut him off. "There are multiple historical documents outside the Bible that make reference to him."

Darlene turned to Chip. "It's not Jesus. It's how they twist his stuff."

"That's right," Amber said. "Jesus, he was like a good teacher—right, Uncle Will?"

I'd done my best to avoid the conflict, not because I was a coward, though there was that, but when compared to these women's fleet-footed communication skills, I was a slow, lumbering mastodon. Still, with every head turning in my direction, I had no choice.

"Yes," I cleared my throat, "he was a good teacher." Seeing I had their full attention, I took the opportunity to expound upon my insight. "A *very* good teacher." There, I said it. I'd taken my stand.

Which was met with Chip's studious response, "More corn bread, please?"

"Actually, that's not correct," Patricia said.

Of course it isn't, I thought while passing Chip the bread and retreating back to my silence.

She continued, "No good teacher walks around claiming to be God. A mental patient, perhaps. A con artist, certainly. But not 'a good teacher.' One would have to agree with C. S. Lewis when he said, Jesus was either a liar, a lunatic, or exactly who he claimed to be: the Lord."

"Butter?" I asked Chip.

He didn't answer. In fact, no one spoke, or ate—or moved. Except for Yeshua who suddenly appeared on the other side of the table.

"Quite a discussion," he said.

I made sure everyone was frozen, before answering. "I hate this."

"Hate?" he reached past Chip to grab some corn bread.

"All the speculation, my lectures, these arguments. Why don't you just show up and be done with it?"

"Tried that once." He bit into the cornbread and began chewing. "Didn't work out so well. Boy, can that woman cook."

"I was perfectly happy just hanging out with you. Just you and me."

He threw me a look.

"Well, *mostly* happy."

He swallowed and took another bite. "It's not just about *you* being happy."

"I know, I know," I said, motioning to the table. "It's all about others." I heard water splashing and turned to see we were suddenly in another dining room; one I'd visited earlier, back when Yeshua had his last meal with the disciples. As before, their faces were lit by a few flickering lamps. The smell of cooked meat, onion, and other spices filled the air. But this time, instead of sitting at the low table, Yeshua, a second Yeshua, was kneeling at the feet of one of his followers. He'd removed the man's sandals and, stripped naked with only a towel around his waist, he was bent over, washing the man's feet in a clay basin.

"What do you see?" the Yeshua beside me asked.

"This is where you wash their feet," I said.

He motioned me to follow him and we stepped closer. "The custom is for the host to wash the guests' feet. But since we had no host, everyone figured the honor would fall to the biggest loser of the group."

"Who was . . .?"

"You told me you've been reading the accounts."

"A twelve-way tie?"

He chuckled and we knelt closer. "During the meal everyone was guessing who'd get stuck with the job."

"And you put their mind to rest."

He nodded. *No servant is above his master.* By serving them, I hoped they'd catch on and start serving others."

"Which," I slowly nodded, "you've been having me do these past few days."

"And brilliantly, I might add."

I frowned, wondering whose life he'd been watching.

The foot washing continued and I was struck by how meticulous the other Yeshua was, as he carefully worked his fingers between each of the man's toes.

"Odd," I whispered. "When I read this, I figured it was more a ceremonial thing; you know, just pouring water over their feet."

"Have you ever known me to leave anything half-clean?"

Good point.

We watched as the other Yeshua lifted the man's foot out of the basin, dried it off, and set the other in the darkened water.

"That's a lot of dirt," I said.

"Dust, dirt, some manure—everything he walked through today."

"Not the perfect dining ambiance."

"Making disciples gets your hands dirty."

"I understand. But . . . how am I supposed to know whose feet to wash? Who's right, who's wrong? With so many opinions and issues and beliefs, how do I choose?"

"That's my job."

"Then what's mine?"

"Love."

"But," I argued, "there's evil in the world, gross wrong-doing. And no amount of group-hugs will fix that."

He motioned to the feet of the man in front of us. "Recognize him?"

I squinted up into the man's face. "Is that . . ." I'd only seen him once or twice but took a guess. "Is that Judas?"

Yeshua nodded, his eyes growing shiny with moisture.

I pressed my point. "So, I'm never supposed to judge? Just wash everybody's feet and ignore the truth?"

He motioned to Judas. "Did I ignore him?"

"No, you called him out. Just like you did that rich kid who wouldn't sell his possessions for the poor."

"I told them just enough truth . . . and then I died for them."

"Truth *and* grace," I said, thinking it through. "Love's double-edged sword."

"That's right."

I continued piecing it together. "The Bible, your Word, that's the truth."

He nodded. "But without my Spirit the Word can . . .?"

"Kill," I said, then quoted a past discussion, "*The letter kills but the Spirit gives life.*"

"That's right. Before acting, wait on my Spirit to hear the deeper."

"The deeper?"

"Put aside your surface logic and wait for me."

"So we're back to that rich kid," I said. "Or even Judas. Waiting on you before we start yanking at weeds and wheat."

"Waiting to hear with my infinite heart—instead of your limited mind."

I blew out a breath of frustration. "That's not much help right now. I mean, what's the bottom line here with Cindy? Or Patricia and Darlene? Who's right, who's wrong?"

"My Word is absolute. True and holy."

"So, Patricia, she's always right?"

"And my love is perfect."

"So she's wrong?"

Smiling at my confusion, he asked, "Would you like to see what I see?"

"Of course!"

Immediately, we were back in my dining room. But this time, with some very different guests.

EIGHTEEN

THE TABLE WAS surrounded by children. I'm no expert, but I'm guessing they were between five and seven years old. It was the same dining room, same table, same food. Only the guests were different. Except for Billie-Jean—who remained in her bassinet cooing and gurgling—every adult was replaced by a child.

"Where'd they go?" I asked.

Yeshua, who stood beaming down at them, replied, "You wanted to see what I see."

I frowned, scanning their young faces as they ate. No one spoke, not a word. Yeshua motioned to the nearest girl, her back to me. I moved to her side for a better look. She was a chubby kid with red, curly hair. There was something strangely familiar about her, especially in the eyes. And she was sitting where Darlene had sat before. Was it possible?

I looked back to Yeshua, "Is that, is this . . ."

He nodded. "Darlene as a child."

"This is how you see her?"

"Your bodies get older, but the core of who you are, your soul—before you disguise it—this is how we see you."

"Little kids locked inside adult bodies?"

"Our precious children," he corrected.

I nodded. Directly across from Darlene sat another girl—blonde, awkward, all knees and elbows.

"Is that . . . Patricia?"

He smiled down at her and nodded.

"And beside her?" I motioned to a geeky kid with glasses. "Chip?"

"No."

"If not Chip, then—" I slowed to a stop, remembering the few family photos my mother took. "That's . . . me?"

"Yes."

I wasn't thrilled at what I saw, but considering the outcome, I wasn't entirely surprised. I motioned toward the only other boy at the table—skinny, thick black hair, and not bad looking. "That's Chip."

"Yes."

Next, I pointed to the prettiest girl at the table, sitting to my right. "And Cindy?"

"He nodded."

I recognized the last member immediately. Although slimmer and acne free, she hadn't changed that much over the past eight or nine years. "And Amber."

"That's right."

"Why are they so quiet?" I said. "No one's talking."

He moved along the table, setting an affectionate hand on each shoulder as he passed. "Even at this age they've learned to use words and language to hide their true identity."

"I don't understand."

"You have to listen past the words to hear them."

"How exactly do you hear someone if they're not speaking?"

"But they are speaking. Listen."

I paused and heard nothing except the occasional fork and knife scraping plates.

"Everything's a metaphor. Look back to Darlene," he said. "What do you see?"

I turned to watch. Instead of eating, she moved what tiny portions of food she had to different locations on her plate. Only when she suspected someone was looking did she actually put a bite into her mouth.

"She's not eating," I said.

He motioned for me to keep watching. As I looked on, she silently scooted a tiny portion of black-eyed peas from one side to the other.

Yeshua explained. "All her life, she's been shamed for being overweight."

"But . . ." I motioned to the small portions.

He answered, "She'll eat later—a candy bar stuffed in her dresser, a bag of chips in the closet—which will only add to her self-hatred."

"Self-hatred?" I said. "She's the most self-assured person I know. Not to mention outspoken." I turned to him, but before our eyes even connected, I had my answer. "Because we hide behind our words."

He nodded.

I turned to the younger Amber. Unlike Darlene, she was piling every food available onto her plate and eating as fast as she could.

"This isn't real, right?" I said. "Only how you see her?"

"She's lost both parents and is afraid of what may happen next." We watched as she shoved a huge forkful of turnip greens mixed with black-eyed peas and mashed potatoes into her mouth. "She's unsure of the future and afraid of missing out so . . ."

He let me finish the thought. ". . . she needs to stuff herself with everything she can find." I took another moment before continuing. "So . . . what I hear as selfish and spoiled?"

"Is nothing but her fear."

He let me watch her another moment before motioning to young Chip sitting beside her. The boy stealthily removed a slice of cornbread from his plate and slipped it under the table to Amber.

"And that's her accomplice?" I said.

"Chip loves to give. That's his nature."

I frowned. "You're kidding." Of everyone there, I liked him the least—always on the make, the take, a twenty-first-century Artful Dodger. "Are you sure?"

"He has an issue or two. But underneath . . ." Yeshua motioned back to the boy as he passed Amber a chicken leg.

I shook my head in wonder.

That left another guest—the gangly blonde. I crossed over to who I now knew to be the childhood Patricia. Like Darlene, she also scooted food around her plate. But she wasn't trying to hide it or make it appear eaten. Instead, she was carefully separating it—turnip greens from the mashed potatoes from the chicken—keeping clear, distinct borders around each of the foods. And this time, for me at least, it made perfect sense. Even today Patricia was obsessed with everything being neat and in its place—always on time, meticulously dressed, constantly exercising, not allowing an extra ounce of body fat.

As I watched, Yeshua explained, "Growing up in the jungles of Papua New Guinea was a frightening experience for her—the stress, the day-to-day chaos and changes."

"So," I said, "all of the need she has for rules and order, it's her refuge, a way to feel safe?"

He nodded. "But so many times it conflicts with the very love I want to share with her. A love that can appear wild and out of control."

I looked to him as he continued, "I will not be put into a cage, Will. I'm not some dot-to-dot picture defined by connecting the points. My love, my real love, can be messy."

"Welcome to my life," I said, then stopped as realization dawned. "Is this why you put me in her life?"

"She lives in fear. Everything about her faith is defensive—desperate to keep me neat and in order. And if there's one thing you've learned about me and defense . . ."

"You never play it," I said.

He nodded. "My truth always wins. It may take its time, but it always prevails."

He paused, letting me take it in, before resuming. "But there's one person you haven't listened to. And it's important you hear her before your guest arrives."

"Guest?"

He motioned to the other girl who would someday be my wife. Strangely, I hadn't noticed before, but unlike the others, her hands darted back and forth—grabbing celery with pimento cheese from Amber's plate, sneaking an entire ear of sweet corn from Chip's.

"What's she doing?" I asked.

Yeshua remained silent.

I moved closer to watch as she continued taking—fried green tomatoes and cornbread from Amber. Not to eat. Her own plate was already brimming with food. Instead, she pilfered anything she could get her hands on, then silently stuffed it into a purse beside her.

And my plate, the one belonging to the geek sitting beside her? The kid who seemed so mesmerized by her presence?

Picked clean.

A heaviness filled my chest as I looked to Yeshua, hoping I'd misunderstood—when the doorbell rang. That, and Siggy's manic barking, broke the vision and, once again, everyone sat around the table in their full, adult size.

"You expecting company?" Darlene asked.

I rose, shaking my head, then changed my mind. "Actually, yes."

I can't explain it, but as I crossed to the back door, I knew who it was. And when I opened it to see the GQ Australian with the polo shirt (arms tailored to show frequent visits to the gym), designer jeans, and Photoshopped teeth, I wasn't surprised.

"G'day," he grinned. "You must be Willie." He reached out to shake my hand.

I took it. "And you are?"

"Buster. Cindy's fella. Couple days late, but here I am."

I glanced down to see the Rolex on his wrist.

"Sweetie!" Cindy cried. She leaped to her feet, but appeared so weak, Patricia and Chip rose in case she needed help.

"Cid!" He brushed past me to join them, pulling her into his arms. "I missed you, girl."

"Me too." She buried her face into his neck, starting to weep. "I was afraid you wouldn't come."

"Me?" he said between kisses. "Got hung up, that's all. But I'm here now." Another kiss, long and heartfelt.

Yes sir, it was a touching sight. Everyone was moved by the lovers' reunion. Even I might have been if one of them had not been my ex. And if I hadn't noticed the sleek, deluxe SUV now parked in the driveway.

PART THREE

NINETEEN

"IT'S A RENTAL. I swear to God."

"And that makes a difference because . . .?"

Amber tried to step in. "Uncle Will."

"Stay out of this." My abrupt tone stopped her.

I had waited until the others left, letting Buster charm and regale them with stories of their world travels. And there wasn't one of them who didn't buy into it, into him—including his story of how their credit cards were hacked and identities stolen.

"Hard stuff," Darlene admitted.

"You have no idea," Cindy said.

And never to be left out of a conversation, Chip added, "I had a friend that happened to once." We looked to him waiting for more but that's all he had.

Sitting around the living room drinking coffee (or in Patricia's case, green tea)—it was London this, Tokyo that, hiking the Himalayas, nearly meeting the president of Nepal—as Cindy sat beside him, the willing accomplice.

Did I believe any of it? It doesn't matter. I sat on the sofa, biding my time, swallowing my anger—like Yeshua with Judas, caring too much for Cindy to call her out in front of friends. I waited until Patricia and Darlene said their goodbyes and headed for their cars to catch the last ferry, before shutting the kitchen door and turning to Buster. "You have no money but you can rent an SUV? Do I look that stupid? What is it a Lexus, Mercedes?"

"C'mon, mate." Buster grinned, thinking his charm still had power. "It's not what you think. You're jumpin' way ahead of your—"

"That's enough!" I brushed past him and headed into the dining room. "You can spend the night . . . on the floor, but after that—"

"The floor?" he scoffed.

"Last ferry's gone, but I want you on the first one tomorrow morning."

"Will?" Cindy said.

"Both of you."

She broke into a fit of coughing—legit or planned, I couldn't tell.

"You call this Christian charity?" Buster said.

Chip chimed in. "He's got a point, Will. If I were you, I'd—"

I cut him a look and he stopped talking. A first as far as I could remember.

I turned back to Buster. "I've been lied to long enough. It's over."

"What did we lie to you about?" he said.

I snorted, seeing no need to dignify the question.

Cindy explained, "I told Will we were broke, that we had no place to stay."

"Broke?" Buster laughed. "We could buy this place three times over."

"With what?" I shot back, "hacked credit cards?"

"I was shootin' straight with you; we can't use 'em."

"Right." I headed into the family room.

They followed, slower as Cindy leaned on him. "We made some people on the mainland a little angry," she said.

"People?"

"We just need some place to stay until I can smooth things over," Buster said.

"There are thousands of motels on the mainland."

"Which only take credit cards, which can be traced," Cindy said.

The room grew silent. "Traced?" I repeated.

She looked away.

Chip tried to hide his excitement. "Like cops or feds or something?"

"Yes, among others," Cindy said.

"Others?" My pulse pounded in my ears. "And you came here? You've come into my house, endangering my niece, her baby."

"Nobody's endangering—"

"Tomorrow. First ferry."

"But, Will," Chip argued. "If they're hiding—"

"And you," I said, "home."

He turned to Amber for a reprieve.

"Now." My voice was low and steel-hard.

Keeping an eye on me, she gave him the slightest nod.

"Alright, fine." Chip kissed her on the forehead.

"Go," I repeated.

"Aright, fine. I'm out of here." He headed for the kitchen door.

"And kid," Buster called. "Don't tell anyone."

"Of course," Chip said, "We're cool."

I motioned to the hallway. "Blankets in the closet. There's a futon in the nursery, buried under all the baby gifts."

෴

Whether Chip told his buddies to impress them was anybody's guess. It didn't matter. Well, maybe a little. I'd hate to see Cindy hurt. Even now. True to my word (somebody had to be true) I insisted Boy Toy sleep on the floor not ten feet from my own sofa/bed. Being a good five inches taller and forty pounds heavier, he could have refused but Cindy's persuasive abilities didn't end with just me.

Come morning, few words were spoken. Not that Buster didn't try, but I was in no mood to reply. And Cindy? I think she was too embarrassed, or maybe ashamed. While packing, she did manage to gather a few extra items from the back of the closet—clothes I'd still not been able to throw away. And Amber talked them into letting her fix them some fried tofu and other concoctions she called breakfast. (*Vengeance is mine*, saith the Lord.)

Later, on their final trip down the hall, Cindy passed her beloved cat—who loathed me as much as I loathed him.

"Mind if I take Karl?" she asked.

"Please," I said.

But when she tried to pick him up, he squirmed, growled, and scampered from her arms—a better judge of character than me.

"Well, mate, wish us luck," Buster said standing at the back door. He extended his hand. I saw no reason to take it. He pulled Cindy closer under one of his big arms. She didn't look up.

"Hold it, wait a minute," I said.

I turned and shuffled down the hall into the laundry room/bedroom/office/guest bedroom. The bed was left unmade. I felt behind the dryer for the Pringles can and dragged it out. Opening the lid, I pulled out two, one-hundred-dollar bills. I hesitated, then pulled out a third before replacing the lid and returning the can.

When I re-entered the kitchen, they'd already opened the back door. I reached past Buster for Cindy's hand. She let me take it and wasn't entirely surprised when she felt the money slip into her palm. Without looking at it, she raised her shiny, red-rimmed eyes to meet mine. Like me, she wanted to say something. But what could be said?

"And off we go." Buster turned and moved them through the door.

"Bye, Aunt Cindy."

She turned back to see Amber, Siggy, and me standing at the counter. She smiled faintly then turned to let Buster help her across the driveway to their SUV. I stepped into the doorway to watch, feeling my throat tighten. He helped her up into the vehicle and carefully buckled her in. Shutting her door, he crossed to his side and climbed behind the wheel. He fired up the engine then turned and gave me what may have been a slight nod.

The sun was diffused by the early morning mist, glimmering low through the trees as he dropped the vehicle into gear and started up the driveway. I continued watching, the tightness in my throat spreading down into my chest. Yeshua said earlier, one way to test our motives was if acting on them was the last thing we wanted to do. I reached for the door, bracing myself as the SUV pull out onto the highway.

And Cindy? She never turned, she never looked back.

How long I stood there, I'm not sure. But the vehicle was well out of sight when I felt a hand resting on my shoulder. And the words. Just three of them, as soft as the morning mist, but just as real:

Truth and grace.

CHAPTER
TWENTY

CLASS WAS EASILY three times the size of Friday's; the usual suspects and more. Tag and Hatchet brought a couple friends, also black, to join them along the left wall. The same was true for PK and Anointed who brought a few of their Latino buddies to hold up the opposite wall. But the largest increase congregated at the back—a dozen men, all white, with the majority sporting provocative tattoos of Nazi crosses, spiderwebs, and SS bolts.

If Yeshua wanted a mosaic of people, he got mosaic.

And if I wanted protection, well, I was grateful for the return of the guard they brought in earlier to join my NBA friend. Her name tag read, Bowers. At first glance, her low center of gravity made her appear short and dumpy. But a closer look at the broad shoulders and thick, bulldog neck said she was not someone to mess with.

When I greeted the group and mentioned the increased size, Tag spoke up. "It is in response to what we witnessed Sunday—you spending the night with Sparky."

Apparently, the doctor's request for me to take the scenic route was more than whimsy.

Anointed called from the other side of the room. "When, Lord, did we see thee hungry and feed thee, or thirsty and give thee drink, or—"

"Sit," PK ordered.

He continued, ". . . in prison and visit—"

"Now."

Anointed sat.

"He's right." It was a hunkering white man from the back. He had the same intimidating build as Hatchet, only with two hands. Like many of his companions, he was bald but he also had a large swastika tatted across the top of his skull. "People come 'round slinging their religion just to make themselves feel good."

Tag pointed at me. "But you, you heard of the despicable actions performed upon him by Hector Hernandez, and you chose to step up."

"Whoa, whoa, whoa," PK called from the Latino side. "You talkin' trash 'bout my man?"

"Not just him, bean dip," one of the whites called back.

Tag nodded. "What he did to Sparky was reprehensible, but no surprise considering his genetic predisposition."

PK stiffened. "His what?"

"Look it up."

"Has to do with your momma," the hunkering white called.

A faint chuckle rippled through the room, to which Hatch added, "And whatever curb-crawler did her that night."

"Which one," Tag said. "There are so many to choose from."

PK rose to his feet, kicking back his chair.

Tag also stood—arms out, palms open, indicating he was ready for whatever PK had in mind. Hatchet joined him. Both guards stepped from their respective walls, a not-so-subtle reminder of their presence.

The hulking white guy called out, "Somebody shoulda' capped Hernandez long ago."

Murmurs of approval.

Tag looked to PK. "Maybe somebody will." Then grinning, he added, "What goes round comes around. Right, amigo?"

The NBA guard finally spoke up. "Okay, gentlemen. It appears class has finished early for the day."

"No man," one of the whites from the back called. Another agreed, "It's good, we're cool."

"Yeah?" the guard said. "Then I suggest you pay attention to what Preacher Man has to say." He stepped back to his wall. "And keep your opinions about Hernandez to yourself." Throwing PK a look, he added, "No matter how accurate they are."

PK shot him a glare.

"His times comin'," one of Tag's men shouted.

"Just a matter of time," the other agreed.

Still holding PK's look, the guard said, "You going to stand down, son, or do we need a little one-on-one?"

PK relaxed, folding his arms. Resigned but not defeated.

The guard motioned for me to continue and I cleared my throat. "Okay, then. The, uh, the last time we met, we were addressing the issue of *imago Dei*."

"Yeah," Hatch said. "Love and all that—" He caught himself, clearly for my benefit. (I saw no need to mention I worked with college kids.)

"Excrement," Tag offered.

"Yeah," Hatch said, "excrement."

"I am love," Anointed called from across the room.

Tag scoffed. "A construct preached by Europeans to keep the black man in chains." Turning back to me, he repeated Friday's argument, "One plus one equals two. That's how the world's run and that's how—"

He was interrupted by an alarm—loud and pulsing, like I heard my first day. The men shouted complaints and obscenities as Bowers quickly strode to the steel green door, slid it shut, and locked it with her set of keys.

"Alright," her partner shouted. "You know the drill."

More oaths as the men lowered to their knees.

"Let's go, let's go," he yelled as they began lying, face down, on the floor.

Bowers reached for her phone.

"What's going on?" I shouted.

"Lockdown!" the tall guard yelled. He motioned for me to join Bowers near the door. As I obeyed, he spotted Tag looking up and grinning. "You find this amusing?"

"No, sir."

"Then face down!"

Bowers shouted what she'd just heard from her phone. "Someone took down Hernandez."

Heads raised, many turning to Tag.

"Not me," he yelled. He looked to PK with a smirk. "I'm right here."

PK rose to his knees. "You called it!"

"Down!" the guard shouted.

"From in here?" Tag yelled. "How's that possible, cholo?"

PK rose to his feet. Others took his cue.

Tag and his men followed suit.

"Everyone down!" the guard shouted.

Tag grinned and yelled, "Payback time."

Instantly, PK broke from his side of the room, rushing at him.

But reading the situation, the NBA guard had already moved to the center. Pulling the baton from his belt, his first swing caught PK in the gut. It took one more across the shoulders, and another into his chest, to stop him.

Hatch rushed in to finish the job but the guard spun around to confront him. Hatch slowed, evaluating the situation. As he did, two of PK's men raced at the guard from behind.

"Look out!" Bowers shouted.

Before her partner could turn, the men tackled him. One threw him into a choke hold as the other scrambled after the fallen baton, scooping it up just a second before Hatch could reach it.

The powder keg had blown. Tag's men rushed in. So did the whites.

Shouting inmates and the pulsing alarm filled the room. Bowers yelled into her phone for backup. PK's man, the one who'd scooped up the baton, raced at Tag—a suicide mission as he had to first go through Hatch.

Meanwhile, one of the whites climbed a chair and was smashing the surveillance camera. Others went after Tag and the blacks. And, being equal opportunity racists, the rest attacked PK's Latinos.

Fists flew—along with plenty of kicking and biting. I ducked a sailing chair just as the lights went out. The emergency lights in the far corner kicked in, reducing the mayhem to blinding brightness and black shadow.

Bowers left the door to assist her fallen partner— working her way to him, swinging her baton, landing several blows.

Across the room, Anointed was shouting, "Brothers! Those who live by the sword—"

Someone hit him with a chair. He stopped talking. After the second blow, he stopped standing.

I worked my way around the chaos to the door, the safest place in the room—until the pounding began on the other side. I thought, I hoped, it was more guards coming—until I heard the voices—thick, Hispanic accents swearing, shouting for Tag and his demise. The pounding was relentless, accompanied by stronger, heavier blows . . . until the door began to buckle.

TWENTY-ONE

"AWAY FROM THE door!" Bowers shouted at me as she knelt beside her partner on the floor. Someone had used his baton on him, striking his head more than once. "Stand back!"

But stand where? The room was filled with flying fists (and chairs). I scooted along the wall, five, six feet when the door started giving way—pushed and pried, creaking and groaning—until it opened just enough for a body to squeeze through. In the light and shadow I saw a short man, bald head wrapped in a bandana. I guessed Hispanic. I stayed pressed against the wall, watching two more squeeze through.

Squinting from the light, the first man shouted over the alarm, *"Donde esta! Donde esta!"*

"Ahi!" Another pointed at Tag, whose back was to them, holding PK off with a homemade knife.

The three raced at him.

One of Tag's men saw them and shouted, "Look out!"

Tag spun around, swinging his knife just in time to catch the first attacker, ripping into his shirt and forcing the others back. "Hatch!" he called over his shoulder. "Hatch!"

Hatch turned and quickly joined his side—drawing two of his own attackers with him. It was now five on two, Tag and Hatch the minority. PK and his men circled them, held back only by Hatch's size and Tag's knife.

"You want payback, boy?" PK taunted. "Here it is."

Tag searched the melee—whites on blacks, blacks on Latinos, Latinos on whites—each fueled by hate and vendettas—until his eyes caught mine. Without a word, he broke toward me, swinging his knife like a machete, clearing the way through PK's men until he arrived and yanked me from the wall.

I shouted, "What are you—"

He slipped behind me, shoving the blade against my throat—not cutting me, but firm enough to mean business. "Stay back!" he yelled. "I'll kill him!"

"Preacher man?" PK laughed and swore. "You ain't killing no preacher."

I felt no need to correct him.

He and his men started toward us until I felt a sharp burn under my chin. Not deep, more like a razor nick, but drawing enough blood to stop them. I strained, looking down. I couldn't see the blade but I did see the smear of blood on Tag's knuckles and the back of his hand.

PK laughed. "You crazy!"

"Your call, cholo." Tag sounded cool and calm, but I felt the rapid rising and falling of his chest against my back.

PK hesitated. Tag took the moment to drag me to the door. I thought of resisting, but the knife suggested otherwise.

"No place to run!" One of the Hispanics shouted. "Hernandez, he ain't dead. And your *puto* assassin, he spilled the beans."

Another laughed. "Before we spilled his guts."

PK grinned at Tag. "What goes 'round comes 'round, right, boy?"

Tag motioned for Hatch to cover us. The big man stepped in to block the attackers as Tag turned and squeezed the two of us through the door. Hatch followed, backing up, never turning his back on them. But our escape was short-lived. On the other side of the door, in the dark hallway, stood a half dozen other inmates, several sporting bandanas—poised and waiting.

"Stay back!" Tag shouted. He pressed the blade harder against my throat. "I'll kill him, I'll kill the preacher."

The men traded looks. The overhead sprinklers kicked on adding to the confusion.

"Tag!" A guard's voice shouted from down the hall, barely heard over the alarm, the sprinklers, the cursing. Impossible to see through the downpour. "What are you doing?"

"Stamph!" Tag yelled. "I want to see Stamph!"

One of the men sneered, "He ain't helpin' you this time." He motioned behind us. We turned and saw PK entering through the narrow opening, followed by others.

"Put the blade down," the guard shouted. "Put the blade down and we'll talk."

"Yeah," PK mocked as he edged toward us. "Then you and me, we can have a nice long chat."

It sounded good to me, but Tag had other ideas.

He dragged me to the side of the hall. Hatch followed, PK's men tracking with us, as close as they dared. We stopped at a side door. With Hatch providing cover, Tag kicked the exit bar and the door flew open. We staggered into the bright sunlight of the small courtyard; Hatch right behind, followed by PK and friends—those from the hallway and those continuing to stream out of the library.

As they spread out, encircling us, Tag leaned to my ear. "You okay, Preacher?"

I tried pulling away, to better answer, or at least distance my carotid artery from his knife, but he'd have none of it.

"Relax, you're just my protection."

I strained to see the knife.

"For negotiation. I won't hurt you." Before I considered relaxing, he added, "Unless I have to."

Strange. But even now something was starting to happen. Instead of my usual, go-to emotions of worry and fear, I began feeling something else. A certain pity. Compassion over the impossible situation he'd gotten himself into. Don't misunderstand me, we weren't becoming BFFs, but some part of me wanted to help. And, no, it wasn't Stockholm Syndrome or any of that. It was deeper.

"Tag!" A voice shouted through a blowhorn from above.

We looked, squinting against the sun just cresting over the two-story structure.

"It's Stamph!" Hatch pointed to an open window above us and to the left.

"What're you up to this time?" Stamph shouted.

"Apparently a misunderstanding," Tag called back.

"Seems you got yourself a little problem."

"How's that?" Tag shouted, moving us around for a better look.

"Hernandez."

"I heard he had an accident."

"Nothin' life-threatening. Can't say the same for his attacker. You knew Youngren, right? One of your boys."

Tag swore under his breath. "I had nothing to do with that," he shouted. "I was in the library."

A red light briefly flared in my eyes. I squinted then spotted a ruby-red dot moving across Tag's arm. I strained as far back as possible as it came to a quivering stop on his forehead . . . six inches from my own face. I turned, searching until I spotted the sniper on the rooftop.

"Put the shank down, Tag," Stamph ordered.

"And then what?" Tag yelled.

"Then we can talk."

Tag motioned to the men surrounding us. "What about the taco eaters?"

"Come on, *boy*," PK taunted. "You can trust us."

"Put it down," Stamph repeated.

Tag moved the knife higher, against my chin, forcing me to raise my head so Stamph could get a better view of the blade. "Shoot me and he's dead."

"Soon as you hit the ground, we'll be there to stop him bleeding out."

Bleeding out! I was not happy with the direction of the conversation.

Tag pulled the knife from my throat and dropped it to my chest, pressing the point into my ribs just over my heart. "And your doctor," he shouted. "She good at doin' transplants?" He was breathing faster.

"Tag," I whispered, "maybe—"

He pressed the point harder. "Shut up!"

It seemed a good idea.

"Alright," Stamph shouted. "Take it easy. You okay, Professor?"

"Yes," I half-whispered.

"Louder," Tag hissed.

"Yes," I croaked. "Yes!"

"Okay, then," Stamph said. "We'll meet and talk."

The knife's pressure decreased slightly.

"Where?" Stamph asked.

Tag searched the courtyard then shouted. "The cafeteria! Just you and me. And tell these cholos to stand down."

"Alright, then," Stamph said. "PK, you heard the man."

Neither PK nor his men liked the idea.

"Let him pass," Stamph repeated. "Stand down."

They heard him. Whether they would obey was another matter.

"My last warning, gentlemen. Stand down."

Finally, PK gave a nod. The men grudgingly stepped aside, leaving a safe passage to the cafeteria door.

It would have been safer if the door was unlocked. Safer still, if PK and his men hadn't noticed that and taken the opportunity to begin closing in. Tag kicked at the door with his foot. Nothing. He tried again. Still nothing—except PK and his men smirking over the realization Tag was cornered.

Once again Hatch turned to defend us, but with a dozen men—and more entering the courtyard from the hallway. It was just a matter of time.

"Stamph!" Tag shouted, "Stamph!"

But Stamph had already left the window to go downstairs.

"Let him go," PK said. "Let Preacher Man go and we'll talk. Mano e cockroach."

"Stamph!"

And then we heard three distinct clicks—the cafeteria door being unlocked, courtesy of two guards. Once they opened it, Tag ducked inside, dragging me with him, making it clear to the guards he still had the knife and their drawn batons would do little good . . . unless they wanted a dead preacher on their hands.

TWENTY-TWO

HATCH STAYED AT the door working with the guards; a fool's attempt to hold off PK's men as Tag dragged me into the cafeteria with its thirty or so steel tables and benches bolted to the floor. His breath came even faster and shorter as he searched the two hallway doors waiting for Stamph's entrance. But the guards were no match for PK and friends. They were quickly overpowered, relieved of their batons which, in turn, were used on them. Hatch fared little better, although it took four blows to drop him.

Tag continued backing up until we were against a long serving counter. By now I counted nearly two dozen of PK's men. Two dozen versus Tag and me. Not great odds, although I hoped the knife pressed into me still put Tag in the majority.

The party had barely started before the farthest hallway door flew open. Not Stamph, but recruits for Tag. The two groups spotted one another and, with about equal number, raced toward each other, their shouts rising to a roar as they met head-on with rage and fury—years of hatred unleashed as they punched and tackled, grappled and gouged. It was no longer the minor skirmish in the library; this was a riot, all-out war. Earlier, Stamph spoke to me about tensions building. It finally had reached critical mass.

Realizing he was no longer the center of attention, Tag eased the knife's pressure. It was clear he wanted to join the mayhem, but equally clear I was still his best life insurance. One of his men leaped over the counter behind us and grabbed a metal colander. He used it to bang on the locks of a nearby drawer.

"What are you doing?" Tag shouted.

"Knives!" the man yelled. "It's where they keep the knives!"

I couldn't help thinking, if this is war, he just introduced the arms race.

I turned back to the fighting. Only now they weren't men fighting. They were little boys! The same age as my guests at last night's supper. I shut my eyes, forcing the vision away. But when I reopened them, they were still there. Some continued fighting, but several sat on the floor terrified, hugging their knees, rocking back and forth, trying to make it go away. Others stood confused, unsure what to do. Lost. Abandoned.

I felt my throat tighten. As with Tag, I felt pity, a compassion rising inside me. If there was some way to help them, something I could do . . .

Out of your heart will flow rivers of living water.

Was this what he meant? Was this—

Someone tackled us from the side. We hit the floor. Tag's knife was knocked from his hand, the back of my head slamming so hard into the counter I lost consciousness.

When I opened my eyes, Tag was gone. Thankfully, so was the knife. The frightened children had become men again. The room returned to its roaring hatred. Only my feeling remained—and continued growing. The deep sorrow. The compassion.

As I tried to rise, struggling to my hands and knees, I heard loud clattering above me. Men from both sides turned, then broke into a run toward me and the sound. I looked up, craning my neck until I saw the reason. The cutlery drawer was finally opened and dozens of knives were strewn across the counter.

Anointed was one of the first to arrive. He scooped up a large butcher knife. Looking down at me he grinned, and quoted, "Those who live by the sword," then turned and disappeared back into battle.

Grabbing the counter, I pulled myself to my feet. I barely managed to stand, the room still shifting, when I heard the *pop* of a rifle. Two more followed as canisters flew into the crowd, clattering to the floor, spinning and spewing gray smoke.

"Gas!" Someone shouted.

The men coughed, covering their eyes. Some pulled up shirts to cover their mouths and noses—as the clouds rose and spread through the room. My eyes began burning, the back of my throat catching fire, forcing me to cough and gag.

Another group entered from the other door. Through watery eyes, I saw the other men from the library pouring in—the whites. Men, yes. But somehow they were little boys as well. Equally lost. Equally terrified. A sob escaped from somewhere deep inside me. It may have been the gas, but I have my doubts. I leaned against the counter, looking down, trying to understand.

When I looked up, I spotted Tag. He did not see the man racing at him from behind; nor did he see the large, carving knife in his hand.

"No!" I shouted. I shoved off the counter and threw myself toward Tag to push him out of the way. I stumbled, but managed to fall into him, wrapping my arms around him, shielding him from the knife . . . as it plunged into my back, between my ribs.

I slid to the floor, pain so deep and hot I couldn't move. I couldn't breathe. I tried to cry out but no sound would come. I could only lie on the floor, watching the feet of the men as they struggled and fought. I convulsed, but not from pain. It was another sob, silent. I had no air to expel. Another followed. Tears streamed down my face. An inmate stumbled over me. I tried to move but could not as the room began growing white. I felt tired. Sleepy. I struggled to keep my eyes open. I closed them, planning to reopen them in just a second.

I was wrong.

Suddenly I sat with Yeshua on the serving counter, wide awake, all pain gone. "What happened?" I cried. "What's going on?"

He motioned to the chaos before us—and the body lying on the floor. I couldn't see the face, but I recognized the shirt and slacks.

"Is that?

He nodded.

"Am I . . . dead?"

"Not yet."

Oddly enough, I felt no panic, no fear. We watched as two more men stumbled over my body, so engaged in fighting they barely noticed. I shook my head, marveling—not that we were looking at my body, but that I felt so little attachment. No more than a pair of worn shoes I'd simply stepped out of. But there was something that did remain. That deep, overwhelming emotion that had been growing . . . that led me to leap between Tag and the knife.

"That was impressive, Will." Yeshua's voice was quiet, a trace of awe.

I shook my head. "But it wasn't me. I mean it felt so . . ." I searched for the word, "natural. Like, how could I do anything else."

He smiled.

"But, how's that possible? Five minutes earlier he was going to kill me."

"Remember what they did to Stephen a few weeks after I died?"

"Stephen . . . the first martyr?"

"The first of millions before you . . . and in years to come."

"They all felt like this? No fear, no regret?"

"Maybe in the beginning . . . until they were overcome by love."

"That's it!" I said. "The whole love thing. I mean I didn't have time to analyze it, but that's what I felt. Like I couldn't help it."

"Love is powerful—so powerful it kept me on the cross."

"Not the nails?"

He simply smiled.

I quietly marveled. "Love. God's love."

He nodded. "And the more time we spend together, the greater it will grow."

"Like a virus," I said. "It just keeps spreading."

He gave me a look.

"No offense."

He grinned. "None taken. Though I do take full responsibility."

Turning back to the men, we noticed Tag had finally spotted my body. He was kneeling at my side, shaking me. When I didn't respond, he raised his head and shouted over the noise, "A doctor! We need the doctor here!"

A handful of men, closest to us, slowed to a stop. They watched as Tag turned me over—the back of my shirt soaked in blood; even more pooling on the floor.

"Get Collins!" he shouted. "Somebody get the doctor!"

More men turned to us, coming to a stop.

"Preacher Man!" someone yelled. "It's the preacher!"

Tag pressed both hands against my bloody back, trying to stop the flow. "Get Collins!"

One of the Latinos knelt beside him as more gathered to watch. There was still fighting along the parameter, but more and more turned, slowing to a stop and watching.

Unable to look away, I asked Yeshua, "They're stopping because of . . . me?"

"Your death will have a powerful impact."

"So I *am* dying."

"It's your choice."

"*My* choice?"

He hopped off the counter. "Come, I want to show you something."

I hesitated, not wanting to leave my body too far behind. "Are we going far?" I asked.

"Not at all."

TWENTY-THREE

I SCOOTED OFF the counter to join Yeshua, and the moment my feet hit the ground I was standing in an aisle at the back of a giant auditorium—so large I could barely see the walls on either side. Walls made of soft, glowing light. Up front, fifty yards ahead, stood a platform carved from the same light yet much brighter. But it was more than light. I can't explain it, but the brightness was also a feeling. A feeling that struck my skin and soaked into my pores. And the more it soaked, the deeper the sensation. Not unlike what I felt when jumping between Tag and the knife.

Not only was it light, it was indescribable love.

On both sides of the aisle stood thousands of people, all smiling, all straining to get a glimpse of . . . me.

"What's going on?" I turned to Yeshua and we were suddenly someplace else—on the opposite sides of a hospital bed. Despite the tubes and hoses, I immediately recognized its occupant.

"How did you do that?" I asked.

"Time's relative, remember?"

It was a typical ICU, not unlike the one my sister died in. Glass enclosed, an IV stand, and a stack of monitors to my right. Except for the *hiss-click, hiss-click* of the respirator, everything was eerily silent.

"How long?" I asked.

"Going on two weeks."

I turned to the heart monitor to see the moving green line and its rhythmic spiking. Not that I'm an expert, but it didn't look bad—until Yeshua explained, "They're keeping you alive."

Like I said, I'm no expert.

And then I heard, "Please Uncle Will . . ."

Immediately recognizing the voice, I turned to see Amber hunched in a chair at the foot of my bed, looking small and helpless. Between choking sobs she cried, "Stop being so selfish. My birthday's next week." With streams of mascara running down her face, she continued, "I need you. Me and Billie-Jean. Please . . ."

I turned to Yeshua who explained, "It'll be hard on her, but she'll survive. Before she's fifty she will have fostered eleven children. And by the end of her life she'll have impacted thousands more people in her church and community."

"Church?"

He simply smiled.

I looked back down as she continued to cry. I thought how even now, at her tender age, she impacted my life— not always intentional or welcomed. But had Amber not shown up on my doorstep Christmas Eve, I would have lived such a . . . well, there was no other word for it, *smaller* life. She was the one who broke me out of my self-made prison, dragging me kicking and screaming into her crazy teen world with its angst-ridden tears and joy—often seconds apart. She was the one who helped me see my unforgiveness toward my father. And, whether she knew it or not, she was the one who brought me to my knees before Yeshua at the cross.

Later, she introduced me to Billie-Jean, forcing me into another, entirely different world—one that involved giving up my life for another. Amazing. Me, the most selfish person on the planet, willing to joyfully (well, usually joyfully) sign up for such a self-sacrificing adventure. Everything from delivering her in the front seat of a hopelessly wrecked automobile, to the impossible-to-describe joy of holding her in the middle of the night, to the raw fear of losing her to a defective heart—while all the time learning the importance of God's version of faith and prayer.

Shaking my head in wonder, I moved around the bed to set my hand on Amber's shoulder in silent gratitude when Yeshua and I were suddenly back in the auditorium with its strange, emotion-filled light. And people. Everywhere I looked grinning, smiling, waving people.

"What is this place?" I asked. "Who are these people?"

"Your cloud of witnesses."

"My what?"

"The ones who've gone before you and have been cheering you on."

"Cheering me on?"

Yeshua cocked his head at me. "You thought you were doing everything by yourself? They've been with you the whole time. Those closest are the ones you know. But as you see, there are thousands and thousands more. And now they're waiting to celebrate." He motioned to the distant platform of light at the end of the aisle. "We've *all* been waiting."

I frowned, trying to understand when we were interrupted by another voice.

"Shut up and show a little respect."

I spun around to see Tag. He sat at his usual place along the wall of the prison library. A library packed with dozens of inmates. One of the tatted-out white guys near the center of the room, shot back, "I'm just saying that if this God is so loving—"

"I get it," Tag said, "and if you'll keep your mouth shut long enough, he'll explain." He turned to the front of the room where Sparky stood with an open Bible on my wobbly music stand.

I turned to Yeshua. "Sparky?!"

Yeshua nodded. "Fifteen months from now."

"He's . . . leading them?"

Yeshua chuckled. "Not well, but he knows his Bible. And, thanks to Tag, not to mention standing up to Hernandez, he's got their respect."

"Tag? Are you saying Tag, is . . .? did he become . . ."

"Intellectual walls and religious pride are tough to breach. But give him time."

I stared at the scene, nearly speechless. "And you're showing this to me because . . ."

"You've finished the race, Will. You can come home."

"Home?"

He motioned behind me and I turned back to the crowd in the auditorium. "Recognize anybody?"

I searched the faces closest to me—distant relatives, forgotten friends, colleagues from work. One young woman in particular stood out to me, her face beaming.

"Is that?" I stepped closer. "When she was young, from her wedding photo . . . is that Mom?"

She clasped her hands, barely able to contain herself.

Yeshua answered, "That's how I've always seen her—even when she was destroying herself with drugs and alcohol."

It became hard to swallow with the lump growing in my throat. She looked so alive, so young and vibrant. And beside her, another face I recognized. Just as young and just as radiant. "Terra!" I cried. "My sister!"

Both women laughed and held out their arms to greet me. I started toward them, but Yeshua held me back. When I looked to him, he shook his head. "Soon," he said. "Not yet."

I turned to the sea of exuberant faces, recognizing many, some as childhood friends, others I suspected to be relatives from long ago. I smiled back, nodding, but began searching for one in particular.

"My dad?" I asked. "Where is Dad?" Yeshua didn't answer. I turned to him. "Where is my dad?"

His face clouded with sadness. He looked away and my heart sank. I had my answer.

We were interrupted by a dog's single bark. I turned again. This time we stood beside a polished, cherry-wood casket. It rested over a freshly dug grave. On the other side of the casket, Reverend Stewart and his wife were quietly comforting Darlene and Patricia. Behind them, in the distance, Amber and Chip walked up a grassy knoll to his car. The boy's arm was around her in a touching display of support. Regardless of my personal dislike for him, which even now seemed to fade, he was always there for her.

The only other attendee was Siggy. He sat beside Darlene and Patricia, staring up at us. He barked again, wagging his tail.

"Can he see us?" I asked.

Yeshua shook his head.

"Then how come he, I mean, he's looking right at us."

"Sometimes animals sense things."

I nodded, then took a moment to look out over the neatly manicured grounds. "Kind of a small turnout."

Yeshua agreed. "The business with your friend, Sean, wasn't that long ago."

Again I nodded, thinking of my close friend who was haunted by his sickness or demons or whatever—and how I stood up for him on an important issue, only to discover I may have been standing on the wrong side. No, not an issue. As Stewart's friend said in church, "There are no issues, only people." And yet it was that standing up, that act of love, no matter how misguided, that helped me discover my identity was not in my work and not in what people thought of me. Instead, as Yeshua was so fond of saying, my identity was being God's "favorite child."

I turned my attention to Patricia. She stood stoically, listening to Stewart's final words. I thought of how much I learned from her: The disciplines so necessary to grow in faith. The courage to stand up for her beliefs. And yet, according to Yeshua, she'd also been learning from me: The fact God doesn't treasure our works as much as our friendship. That any permanent changes in us must come from him—his presence working inside out and not our religious efforts working outside in. While Patricia taught me the discipline of knowing Scripture, Yeshua made it clear the letter devoid of the Spirit can kill, while it's the Holy Spirit of God who gives life.

And finally there was Darlene. Profane, yes. But in so many ways more honest than any of us.

Yeshua read my thoughts and said, "Her insistence upon truth will overcome the abuse and hypocrisy she suffered as a child. And when she returns to the faith of that child, she'll assist others who have traveled that same route."

I nodded and looked over the group. "Only six," I mused. "That's all who showed?"

"On this side, yes," Yeshua said, "but here . . ." He motioned behind us and we turned back to see the eager, waiting faces—as the light continued seeping deeper and deeper into me.

I stood a long moment before Yeshua leaned to me and quietly spoke. "It's your call, my friend."

"More free will?" I asked.

"It's always been about free will. And my love."

"Love," I said. "Truth and grace."

"That's right. It's been a long journey, but now you understand."

I hesitated, then looked back to see Stewart and his wife saying their goodbyes and starting up the hill to their car. Only then did Patricia slump, barely noticeable, as a silent sob shook her body.

"If you stay," Yeshua said, "you'll continue touching lives, displaying my love. But know this, your physical recovery will be long and painful."

I nodded, then stopped. "What about my books? If I leave now I'll never finish writing them."

"Not on paper. But Tag, Sparky, the people you see before you . . . you'll continue writing on their hearts for years to come."

Patricia sobbed again, more openly.

Darlene, her own eyes red and puffy, reached out to her and they embraced.

"It's really my decision?" I asked.

"You've accomplished everything we hoped for, became nearly all we dreamed."

"Nearly?"

He said nothing.

"And if I choose to stay?"

He smiled. "I'm sure we can find something to keep you busy."

That's when I heard the music. Not only heard, but like the light, I felt it—soaking into me. Beautiful voices, highs and lows, intertwining, slowly undulating into one breath-taking chord after another.

I looked to Yeshua. "House band," he said. "Warming up for your arrival."

I turned back to Patricia and Darlene. They took a final moment to gather themselves. Then they turned and, still holding hands, walked up the knoll to their cars.

Only Siggy remained.

"Hey fella," I softly whispered.

He cocked his head at me.

"Siggy!" Chip called from the top of the hill. "Let's go, fella!"

He twitched an ear in Chip's direction, but remained facing me. He gave a soft, mournful whine. So heart-wrenching I had to look away.

Chip opened the car door and called again, "Siggy!"

I looked back to my dog who seemed insistent upon waiting—no matter how long it took.

"Siggy?"

But he couldn't wait forever. I lifted my hand and with a thickening voice said, "Go on, boy." I waved him away, "Go with Chip."

He hesitated.

I cleared my throat and spoke more sternly. "Go on. Go, now."

He cocked his head a final time.

"Go!"

Then, without warning, he turned and trotted off to join Chip and Amber.

"So," Yeshua spoke quietly. "You've made your decision."

Unable to answer, I simply watched Siggy. Apparently, I had. I took a deep breath and blew it out. My eyes brimmed with tears as I felt Yeshua's hand on my shoulder.

And then, the strangest thing happened. Just before we turned, Siggy came to a stop. Midway between the cars and my grave, he turned and abruptly sat.

"Siggy!" Chip called.

But Siggy would not move. He simply stayed there, thumping his tail, looking at me . . . and waiting.

Soli Deo gloria

Insight
Rendezvous with GOD
Volume Four

DISCUSSION QUESTIONS

<u>CHAPTER ONE</u>

1. *I can do all this through him who gives me strength.*
   (Philippians 4:13)

As two country kids moving to Los Angeles from the foot-hills of the Cascades in Washington State, my wife and I were more than a little nervous. Although Paul wrote this in regards to suffering, it is the verse that gave us the courage to keep going. It also came in handy when a misinformed publisher back east asked if I would write a book for them. (Didn't he know I got C's and D's in my one writing class in college?) I was terrified, completely out of my depth. But we were hungry, they offered money—and we had this verse.

Has this verse ever played out in your life? How?

2. Regarding the Bible as literature.

An off-Broadway playwright with an immense ego once told me he turned from atheism to Christianity. When I asked him why, he said, "It's the only book I've read that I couldn't make better." (I did mention he had an ego, right?)

Do you struggle with parts or passages of the Bible? Discuss a few.

CHAPTER TWO

I love the actual account in Matthew 14. How often I'm tempted to look at the wind and waves of my situation, the noisy circumstances that try to distract me from Christ's immovable promises.

1. What are the biggest waves and fiercest gales in your walk? When the storms are at their worst, what is the best way to practice hearing his quiet but absolute Word?

CHAPTER FOUR

1. Once again Will is trapped in binary thinking of whether he should act in truth or in love.

2. Have you been confronted with similar choices?

3. In some dealings do you ever find it easier to deal with the world than with Christians? I appreciate my brothers' and sisters' honesty, their love and gentle kindness, but sometimes I wonder if they are so concerned about hurt feelings, they avoid telling the entire truth and wind up doing more damage than good.

What do you think?

4. Hebrews 10:24 reads, *And let us consider how we may spur one another on toward love and good deeds.*

How do we know when to use the spurs so they help? How can we avoid using them to hurt?

5. Does Yeshua's suggestion offer any help?

CHAPTER FIVE

A couple disclaimer notes:

I'm a sucker for detail and love visiting the locations I write about. (My best job ever was writing the *Fire of Heaven Trilogy* where I convinced the publisher to send me to Israel as well as visiting each of the remains of the seven churches of The Revelation in Turkey. Ah, the good old days. But since I'm allergic to lawsuits by prison officials, this entire institution is fictional. And for that one reader who will gleefully point out Washington State correctional officers don't use batons, I thank you in advance. Kudos to Washington State for making that work. Unfortunately, I couldn't do the same.

CHAPTER SIX

1. *Imago Dei.* Created in the image of God. What if I really believed that? How would my views change if I saw everyone, including vile, evildoers, as being created in his image. Would I behave differently toward them? How?

2. Schizophrenic. An interesting description for those slowly (and sometimes painfully) being transformed into holiness—one minute they're Christ-like, the next, worldly. I remember seeing a book titled, *Caution, Christians Under Construction*. I believe the cover showed a pastor looking up nervously—wearing a hard hat. How much slack would we give each other if we took that concept to heart?

Can you think of a specific person in your own life where it wouldn't hurt to be wearing a hard hat when around them? Does that understanding help you be a bit more patient with them?

CHAPTER SEVEN

1. How sad for folks who think being born again is the end of the process—when it's actually the beginning. It's like getting into a football stadium with our ticket and just sitting there saying, "Here I am, I got the ticket." When in reality Jesus invited us into the stadium so we can go down onto the field and play alongside him.

2. "Growing pains." Maybe this is what James had in mind when he wrote:

   Consider it pure joy, my brothers and sisters, whenever you face trials of many kinds, because you know that the testing of your faith produces perseverance. Let perseverance finish its work so that you may be mature and complete, not lacking anything. (James 1:2–4)

3. What growing pains are you currently undergoing? James tells us to consider it PURE joy. That's a tall order—but easier when we know the ultimate endgame: to be *mature and complete, not lacking anything.*

CHAPTER EIGHT

1. Ah, there it is again—the difference between enabling and helping. Can you think of a couple times you enabled? What was the outcome?

2. And, on the other side, have there been times you've come down too hard on someone? How did that turn out?

CHAPTER NINE

1. Is Will's ignorance a lack of love? Why? Why not?

2. Does your answer have any impact upon our culture? Why? Why not?

3. What is God's solution for being 100 percent just and yet also being 100 percent love?

CHAPTER TEN

1. Like Will, have you ever surprised yourself by being bolder about your faith than you intended? Jesus promised that's what might happen when he said:

> *"But when they arrest you, do not worry about what to say or how to say it. At that time you*

> *will be given what to say, for it will not be you
> speaking, but the Spirit of your Father speaking
> through you."* (Matthew 10:19–20)

2. What are your thoughts regarding Yeshua's mission not being political? Isn't that a cop-out? Was Jesus ever put into a position to comment on politics? What about the time he was challenged to pay taxes? Or take a stand on capital punishment regarding the woman caught in adultery? Did he clearly answer either of those questions?

CHAPTER TWELVE

1. The first time I read Jesus's "**I am**" statement in John 8, I couldn't believe it. He was using the same terminology God used when speaking to Moses from the burning bush. (Little wonder in the next verse, the men picked up stones to kill him.) It was C. S. Lewis who pointed out you can't patronize folks by saying Jesus is a good teacher. Good teachers don't go around claiming to be God. They either have to be a liar, a lunatic, or exactly who he claimed to be—Lord.

2. With Jesus's promises about expecting persecution, do we run the risk of failing to give full disclosure? Are we candy-coating the gospel?

3. How is it possible to have both persecution and peace?

CHAPTER THIRTEEN

1. *"Not everyone who says to me, 'Lord, Lord,' will enter the kingdom of heaven, but only the one who does the will of my Father who is in heaven. Many will say to me on that day, 'Lord, Lord, did we not prophesy in your name and in your name drive out demons and in your name perform many miracles?' Then I will tell them plainly, 'I never knew you. Away from me, you evildoers!'"* (Matthew 7:21–23)

Miller, the inmate, makes a distinction between Christians and followers of Jesus. Is that a fair statement? How does it fit with Jesus's statement in Matthew 7?

2. Take another look at Jesus's provocative parable of the ten virgins in Matthew 25. What was the criteria for them entering the wedding banquet?

CHAPTER FOURTEEN

1. When we stopped being starving artists, my wife and I brought in one of the top ten financial advisors of our state to tell us how to manage money. We had plenty of experience being poor, but having extra change in our pockets was a brand-new thing for us. After a thorough evaluation—including the suggestion we occasionally buy new clothes (which made no sense as my twenty-five-year-old ones fit just fine)—he said, "And be sure to give at least 10 percent of your money away." I said, "Oh, you're a Christian." He said, "That's irrelevant. I tell all my clients that. Giving part of their money away

is always a better investment than if they try to keep it. Don't tell me how it works, it just does." So if you're having trouble believing God on this, feel free to check with our financial guy.

> *"Give, and it will be given to you. A good mea-sure, pressed down, shaken together and running over, will be poured into your lap. For with the measure you use, it will be measured to you."* (Luke 6:38)

2. And not just with money. I play a game with God titled, "Who Can Outgive Who." And, so far, in every cat-egory, he just keeps winning. (I guess he doesn't know how to lose.)

What are your thoughts on giving and God's economy?

CHAPTER FIFTEEN

Whew. "No issues, only people." If I could only hang on to that during my arguments and disagreements. It's certainly no excuse to compromise God's holy Word, no more than it's an excuse to devalue another with whom I disagree.

1. How do we know where to land when we unite *imago Dei* with God's double-edged sword of truth and grace?

CHAPTER SEVENTEEN

> *He has made us competent as ministers of a new covenant—not of the letter but of the Spirit; for*

the letter kills, but the Spirit gives life. (2 Corinthians 3:6)

What an amazing statement, and one that can be misap-
plied both ways:

1. Can you think of an instance where well-meaning
   people, even yourself, have killed using the Word without the direction of the Spirit? Talk about that and how
   it can be redeemed.

2. And the other side? Have there been times we've com-
   promised the Word by confusing human sentimentality
   with the direction of the Spirit? What did that look like
   and how can we do better?

3. So how do we know the difference? As with everything
   else, it seems to come down to our relationship with
   God. We've got the sword of his Word, now we must be
   so intimate in our communion with him, we will only
   wield it in the ways he directs.

CHAPTER EIGHTEEN

A prayer: *Lord, make me so secure in your love that I never feel
threatened by people or their actions. May I always see them
first as your children.*

CHAPTER NINETEEN

Truth and Grace. On the surface they're two opposite
views, but actually come together in God's love. I treasure

God paradoxes. They simply mean I have to, once again, expand my understanding of how great he is.

1. In your opinion, were Will's actions too hasty in asking Cindy and Boy Toy to leave?

2. Did he act too late?

3. Given what he's learning from Yeshua, how would you have had him act?

CHAPTER TWENTY-TWO

1. Can you recall a time you surprised yourself by doing something entirely out of your nature for love? Maybe it was a romance. (I still remember running down my dormitory hallway after my wife agreed to a second date and shouting, "Yes! She said yes!") Or maybe it's that continual self-sacrificing love of a parent for a child. Or, well the list goes on.

2. Imagine what the world would be like if everyone was filled with that love for total strangers—or enemies—or those who want to kill us. If ever there was a way for God's *kingdom to come and his will to be done on earth as it is in heaven*, that would be it.

CHAPTER TWENTY-THREE

1. I love the fact the books Will has been writing may actually be upon people's lives (and not simply on paper or upon computer screens).

2. If you were given the choice Will was given, what would your decision be? Why?

3. As Will would say, it's been quite an adventure. I hope that's been the case for you. It definitely was for me. Instead of my usual approach to writing, which involves praying and then going to work, I tried something different. I tried praying *as* I worked. I'd literally write myself into a corner then turn to the chair I pretend Jesus sits in during my morning devotionals and say, "Now what?" The answers that bubbled up in my head and made it onto these pages were often as surprising to me as some may have been to you. In any case, thanks for sticking with me through this journey. I sure appreciated the company.

In Christ's unfathomable love,

Sneak Peek:

SEER

Rendezvous with GOD
Volume Five

AFTER HIS DEATH, including a tour of heaven, Will realizes Earth's great need and agrees to return to help. With Jesus's instruction and their occasional visits to Old Testament times and prophets our hero learns through failure and mishaps (always with a touch of Myers's humor), how to prepare for the battles God has called him to fight.

Previous Praise for Bill Myers's Novels

Blood of Heaven

"With the chill of a Robin Cooke techno-thriller and the spiritual depth of a C. S. Lewis allegory, this book is a fast-paced, action-packed thriller." —Angela Hunt, *NY Times* best-selling author

"Enjoyable and provocative. I wish I'd thought of it!" —Frank E. Peretti, *This Present Darkness*

Eli

"The always surprising Myers has written another clever and provocative tale." —Booklist

"With this thrilling and ominous tale, Myers continues to shine brightly in speculative fiction based upon biblical truth. Highly recommended." —*Library Journal*

"Myers weaves a deft, affecting tale." —*Publishers Weekly* The Face of God

"Strong writing, edgy . . . replete with action . . ." —*Publishers Weekly*

Fire of Heaven

"I couldn't put the *Fire of Heaven* down. Bill Myers's writing is crisp, fast-paced, provocative . . . A very compelling story." —Francine Rivers, *NY Times* best-selling author

Soul Tracker

"*Soul Tracker* provides a treat for previous fans of the author but also a fitting introduction to those unfamiliar with his work. I'd recommend the book to anyone, initiated or not. But be careful to check your expectations at the door . . . it's not what you think it is." —Brian Reaves, *Fuse* magazine

"Thought provoking and touching, this imaginative tale blends elements of science fiction with Christian theology." —*Library Journal*

"Myers strikes deep into the heart of eternal truth with this imaginative first book of the Soul Tracker series. Readers will be eager for more." —*Romantic Times* magazine

Angel of Wrath

"Bill Myers is a genius." —Lee Stanley, producer, Gridiron Gang

Saving Alpha

"When one of the most creative minds I know gets the best idea he's ever had and turns it into a novel, it's fasten-your- seat-belt time. This one will be talked about for a long time." —Jerry B. Jenkins, author of *Left Behind*

"An original masterpiece." —Dr. Kevin Leman, best-selling author

"If you enjoy white-knuckle, page-turning suspense, with a brilliant blend of cutting-edge apologetics, Saving Alpha will grab you for a long, long time." —Beverly Lewis, *NY Times* best-selling author

"I've never seen a more powerful and timely illustration of the incarnation. Bill Myers has a way of making the gospel accessible and relevant to readers of all ages. I highly recommend this book." —Terri Blackstock, *NY Times* best-selling author

"A brilliant novel that feeds the mind and heart, Saving Alpha belongs at the top of your reading list." —Angela Hunt, *NY Times* best-selling author

"Saving Alpha is a rare combination that is both entertaining and spiritually provocative. It has a message of deep spiritual significance that is highly relevant for these times." —Paul Cedar, Chairman, Mission America Coalition

"Once again Myers takes us into imaginative and intriguing depths, making us feel, think and ponder all at the same time. Relevant and entertaining. Saving Alpha is not to be missed." —James Scott Bell, best-selling author

The Voice

"A crisp, express-train read featuring 3D characters, cinematic settings and action, and, as usual, a premise I wish I'd thought of. Succeeds splendidly! Two thumbs up!" —Frank E. Peretti, *This Present Darkness*

"Nonstop action and a brilliantly crafted young heroine will keep readers engaged as this adventure spins to its thought- provoking conclusion. This book explores the intriguing concept of God's power as not only the creator of the universe, but as its very essence." —Kris Wilson, *CBA* magazine

"It's a real 'what if ?' book with plenty of thrills . . . that will definitely create questions all the way to its thought-provoking finale. The success of Myers's stories is a sweet combination of a believable storyline, intense action, and brilliantly crafted, yet flawed characters." —Dale Lewis, TitleTrakk.com

The Seeing

"Compels the reader to burn through the pages. Cliffhangers abound, and the stakes are raised higher and higher as the story progresses—intense, action-shocking twists!" —Title Trakk.com

When the Last Leaf Falls

"A wonderful novella . . . Any parent will warm to the humorous reminiscences and the loving exasperation of this father for his strong-willed daughter . . . Compelling characters and fresh, vibrant anecdotes of one family's faith journey." —*Publishers Weekly*

Rendezvous with God

"Gritty. Unflinching. In your face. Emotionally wrenching. *Rendezvous with God* is Bill Myers at the top of his imaginative game. A rip-roaring read you can neither tear yourself away from, nor dare experience without thinking." —Jerry Jenkins, *New York Times*-bestselling novelist and author of the Left Behind series

"A teacher and a storyteller, Bill Myers welcomes, disarms, then edifies in this tight and seamless weave of story and truth. It's innovative, 'outside the box,' but that's why it works so well, bringing the reader profound and practical wisdom, the heart of Jesus, in modern, Everyman terms— and always with the quick-draw Myers wit. Jesus talked to me through this book. I was blessed, and from some of my inner shadows, set free. Follow along. Let it minister." —Frank Peretti, *New York Times*-bestselling author of *This Present Darkness*, *The Visitation*, and *Illusion*

"If you have ever wished for a personal encounter with Jesus Christ, *Rendezvous with God* may be the next best thing. Bringing Jesus into contemporary times, Bill Myers shows us what Jesus came to do, and why He had to do it. This little book packs a powerful punch." —Angela Hunt, *New York Times*-bestselling author of *The Jerusalem Road* series

BILL MYERS

Rendezvous with GOD

a novel

"Jesus talked to me through this book.
I was blessed...some of my inner shadows set free."

—FRANK PERETTI, bestselling author of *This Present Darkness*

BILL
MYERS
a novel
Temptation
Rendezvous with God Volume Two

BILL MYERS

a novel

Commune

Rendezvous with God Volume Three